Praise for If or When I Call

"*If or When I Call* is a novel about desperate people shot through with arrows of grace that only a writer as sensitive and insightful as Will Johnson can wield. Lives in small towns are not small, and neither is this author's heart."
> —Wiley Cash, New York Times-bestselling author of
> *The Last Ballad* and *A Land More Kind Than Home*

"*If or When I Call* is a beautiful, masterful, soulful novel. It's truly remarkable that this is Will Johnson's debut book. He writes with the smoothness and assurance of a seasoned veteran, relating a story about ordinary people who are just trying to make a life for themselves, and hoping for a little solace along the way. It's a wonderful ballad, as haunting and brilliant and ultimately redemptive as Johnson's music. This novel is a soaring achievement."
> —Don Lee, author of *Lonesome Lies Before Us*

"What a surprising and brilliant debut novel. *If or When I Call* reads with the urgency of a thriller and weaves seamlessly the story of a broken family as they navigate mental illness, dead end jobs, and lost dreams. Like so many families struggling to survive, it's a tightrope act with no net below. Will Johnson's the real deal, and I couldn't recommend it more. "
> —Willy Vlautin, author of *Don't Skip*
> *Out on Me* and *Lean on Pete*

"Already one of my all-time favorite musicians and songwriters, Will Johnson's first novel shows a natural progression into longer formed prose. *If or When I Call* is a haunting and elegiac look into the lives of small-town, 21st-century America. Simultaneously deeply personal yet near-universal with the most being told in the minute details of the kinds of everyday lives that usually defies novelistic storytelling. Intimate, yet cinematic. As strong a debut novel as I've seen in a very long time.

—Patterson Hood, Drive-By Truckers

"*If or When I Call* is pitch-perfect, about characters far from pitch-perfect, just trying to get a handle on their rudders. Great, great, great."

—George Singleton, author of
You Want More: Selected Stories

"*If or When I Call* is a lyrical and ambitious debut. Johnson gives us a chorus of overlooked voices, exploring the intricate complexities of rural life and family. Heartfelt and heavy."

—Ashleigh Bryant Phillips, author of *Sleepovers*

"With humility and grace, *If or When I Call* sheds a necessary light on folks forever struggling in a place they can't wait to leave and which, when they do leave, remains inescapably inside of them. Will Johnson has written a formally ingenious novel that is both comic and poignant, familiar and mysterious. His confused characters prove resilient in a way that does not seem the least bit contrived. Here is a story that sings, rather than pronounces, its meaningful intentions."

—Michael Parker, author of *Prairie Fever*
and *The Watery Part of the World*

"*If or When I Call* is a tender novel about the brokenness of human nature, and about what it feels like to live with addiction and an undiagnosed illness."

—*Foreword Reviews*

If or When I Call

- a novel -

FOR Jina.
WITH ETERNAL LOVE FOR
YOUR SPIRIT, VOICE, ARTISTRY,
AND FRIENDSHIP.
THANK YOU FOR BEING A
CONSTANT BEACON IN MY LIFE.
ALL BLESSINGS IN
LIFE & ART.
♡, Will

Will Johnson

Printed in the United States of America

First Edition, 2021

ISBN 978-0-9985554-6-1
GMGB03

Cover design by Darin Bradley
Cover image, "Dispatch from Como, Mississippi"
by Matt White
Author photo by Jessie Johnson
Interior layout and design by Aaron Leis

Goliad Media is a production house based in Denton,
TX, showcasing art, literature, music, and mixed media.
We dream of empty places.

goliadmedia.net

For Jessie, and for mom.

Parker

(Blackness. Long breath. Exhale. Static. Long breath again. Exhale again. Static fade. Cold sweat on forehead. Here.)

Apparently I'd thrown an old paint tray. I remember the sound. A clank. As I came to, I could see it was on the other side of the garage now. I sat down on the lip of concrete that separates the washing machine from the rest of the garage. Took four or five deep breaths. Then I went on into the kitchen and got a Gatorade out of the fridge. They were the small ones that tend to hydrate you just enough. Just a dash of sugar. Lectro-lites. Something. I leaned against the counter and heaved another deep breath, then went out through the hall into the living room. I opened the moody sliding glass door that always got off its track, went outside, and sat down in a rusting metal folding chair on the back porch for a few minutes. The sun felt good on my face and arms. The wind blew through the oak trees overhead, and Martin Gattis's black mouth cur, Rosy, stood at the fence. She barked at everything and nothing all the same.

My family's lived here in Rutherford for four generations now. Folks joke that you can see the end of the earth from here. Soybeans, cotton, purple hull peas, and maybe a little rice stretching to the end of the horizon in most every direction. Dad would take me up in his small plane when I was a boy. In the summers our world looked like a patchwork quilt from the air, each square of earth meticulously plowed into parallel and perpendicular rows of varying greens and browns. Stories, gossip, and lives flourish in that rich soil. Dad's been dead eleven years now, and mom four. Pancreatic cancer for him. Lung for her. I've got an older brother in Jackson. In real estate. Or brokerage, to be more accurate. We don't see each other much, but he calls and checks in every now and again. He always said he hated Rutherford and that he'd never be back, and so far that's pretty well held up. Cousins in Sikeston, Perryville, and Festus, and another in Martin, Tennessee. More elsewhere, further east. We've all been farmers, teachers, sales clerks, carpenters, cooks, painters, delivery drivers, servers, maintenance workers, truck drivers, runners, auto body repair folks, alcoholics, zealots, introverts, abusers, do-gooders, and landscapers. Golf cart repair people, too.

I started with the cable company four years ago. Ben's mama and I still laughed and had date nights then. We cooked together and wrestled around and took walks and stayed up late and watched movies. We'd let Ben stay up with us on weekends. Blue glow of the TV in the living room. Something PG-rated.

Melinda and I met seventeen years ago, Christmas. She'd moved to town from Caruthersville to work for her uncle Jerris at The Lantern, a little shotgun-style bar on Wells Street. The bar had been in her family for nearly forty years, and Jerris had run it for the last twenty or so. The Lantern was where me, Shane, Leon and maybe some of the other guys from work would meet a couple times a week. They took a lot of pride in their place and decorated it to the hilt during the holidays. Back then I spent my days driving a truck and delivering washing machines, dryers, deep freezes, stoves, and refrigerators for McCall's, and that night was The Lantern's annual Christmas potluck. Jerris worked the place diligently. He was a man of great detail, and always pretty quiet. He was getting on in his years and was hard of hearing, but you could tell he really looked forward to that time of year. He'd put a big piece of plywood over the pool table, then a red velvet tablecloth over that, and then he and Jenny and Lisa that worked for him would lay out all the food. Lights up everywhere, and usually Curtis Keen at his electric piano in the corner, playing all the classic Christmas songs in a Santa suit that was too big for his frame. Everyone was in a good mood at those things. The bar was usually two, three people deep all the way around, and it stayed that way most of the night. There was usually a meaningless, long-named bowl game on the TV in the corner.

She was tending bar, and Jerris was introducing her to all the regulars. Despite the new surroundings, she had a confidence about her, facing strangers with a lot of history together. She came over. With the fuel of three beers in me, I said who are you and what are you doing in my town?

She said I beg your pardon?
   I said it all again.
   She said I'm Melinda, and extended her hand.

She was only from two towns over, but around here that can be a world away. There was a swirl of noise around us and yet, still an ease about her. She wore faded jeans and a green and black flannel shirt. Red T-shirt underneath, and I remember she had on dark brown, worn-in work boots. Long and straight brown hair. She seemed to float from point to point, unfazed by the chaos of the room. It would become something I'd lean on over the years. Something I'd be in love with no matter how troubled our waters got.

Just moved to town. Helping my uncle here for a while, she said, motioning toward Jerris.

I'm Parker, I said over the noise. I shook her hand.

Well, it's nice to meet you, Parker. Happy holidays.

I hooked my feet under the railing, tensing up. Shane and Leon were looking over at us.

She paused, then said Hang tight, I'm not done with you yet.

Then she turned and went to pour a drink for someone in the fray.

She made her way back over.

What're you drinkin', hon? she asked.

Budweiser.

Want a shot with it?

I'm all right, but thanks.

I didn't really want the beer at this point. I didn't need it. But I didn't care. I owned up to my own want just as an excuse to talk to her.

Leon and Shane kept talking. I was squeezed in between people, hoping for a seat at the bar to open up. She brought the beer over.

What's the story? When'd you start up here?

Just this week. Settling in, helping my uncle for a while.

Well, welcome to town. I sure love this place. We all love Jerris, and I'm glad to meet you, Melinda. Those are my friends Shane and Leon over there. I motioned over. Shane and Leon were oblivious, talking on and on.

You sticking around here for a while? she asked.

We'll probably be here for another beer or so. Depends on what those guys wanna do, I said. They're my ride.

I motioned over to Shane and Leon.

McCall's? she asked.

What?

That patch. On your work shirt. That the appliance store on the square?

Yeah, why?

Need a small fridge. My new place here in town I'm renting doesn't have one and I'm sick of eating out.

All right.

Cool. Hang tight real quick.

She went off and poured a round of Jamesons for three barrel-chested, desk job-looking guys across the bar, then came back and released a few inches of blank receipt paper out of the register.

Here. Write your number down and we can figure something for next week. I need it pretty soon.

I can get you a fridge, I said, excited about a reason to stay in touch.

What? she said.

I said I can get you a fridge.

I scribbled my number down, sliding it across the bar.

All right, hon.

She took the paper and smiled. She folded it carefully and shoved it down into her front left pocket.

I'll call in a day or two, she said.

All right.

Melinda turned to make a gin and tonic for a woman across the way.

For that small minute it felt like some new dawn had taken over.

I was awake and rejuvenated. I felt new.

I miss that version of me. Or us, more specifically.

A seat opened up, so I just sat alone for a moment, nursing the new beer. Shane and Leon talked on and on.

Melinda and I got married eight months later.

Ben came along just after that.

The fits didn't start 'til just a couple years ago. I'd heard from different folks that a body goes through significant changes every seven years or so. I had a series of faint spells as a kid, and low blood pressure through young adulthood. Panic attacks had become more of a thing since fatherhood. None of it prevented me from working. I tried to stay present for my family and friends. I'd taken to building small tables in the garage, just to settle my mind. I'd hand cut everything and just take it slow. That slow assembly became meditative in its way. Melinda would ask questions about the fits, and I did my best to describe them. At least what I remembered.

The first one was at the Sonic. It was just Melinda and me. We'd been out doing errands and Ben was home on his own. We waited in the car for the order. I remembered the sound of the speaker when we were ordering, then the floorboard falling out. I was just hanging there looking down into some canyon for what felt like a mile. Last thing I remember was my mouth moving, and noises coming out, and then there was a gap. I came to on the ride home, and looked over at Melinda driving. I could hear Eric Clapton's "Wonderful Tonight" on the radio low.

Did we eat already? I asked.

She sighed.

I did, she said flatly.

But I didn't? I said.

Yours is in the floor there. In the bag.

Good 'cause I'm hungry.

You can eat when we get home.

We got Ben's? I asked.

Yeah, we got Ben's, she said, becoming more tense.

She leaned her head on her left hand and steered with her right. She sighed again. We were already on the other side of town now, which told me that I'd been out a while.

What went down?

She looked over at me, then back straight ahead.

You don't remember?

No.

You really don't remember any of it?

No.

All the twitching?

No.

All the shit you said about White Tiger this and White Tiger that?

No.

That shit about Paris fucker crypton sucker?

No, Mel—

Well, the crypton sucker part was really something. You don't remember? You just kept screaming it.

I don't.

Ten, twelve times. Loud.

Huh.

Sure got everyone's attention.

It did?

Yeah, three of the Sonic girls came out. All of 'em had their phones in their hands, I can only guess ready to call the cops.

She pulled over in the Jr. Food Mart parking lot, put the car in park, turned the radio off, and turned toward me. She let out another long sigh.

You really don't remember?

I don't, Melinda. I'm sorry.

Any of it?

No.

She turned back and looked over St. Francis street. A few sprinkles started to hit the windshield. Then she looked back across at me.

All right, Parker.

All right, what?

Let's get on home.

But did anyone-?

Did anyone what? she said, putting the car into drive, checking for traffic over her left shoulder.

Never mind.

Let's get on home, she said. You need to eat.

Melinda turned the radio back on. The Clapton song was in the outro by now. We rode along St. Francis for another minute, then took a left on Mays Street. By then the rain started to come down a little more. I sunk down in the car seat and looked up through the canopy of trees passing over us as we drove along. Over the smell of the two warm Sonic bags at my feet, I thought to myself how much I'd always hated that Clapton song.

Melinda

I held it together for a long time. I was patient. At least I think I was. But we'd been out of step for most of those last two years. Orbiting around one another, gradually reduced to a couple of flatlining roommates. It got to where it seemed like any little thing could set us off. I'd pick on how he'd put the dishes in the dishwasher. He'd pick at my smoking. I'd pick back at his. He'd pick at how I drove. I'd pick at all his time spent in the garage hidden away, working on god knows what. Then he'd pick at my not dressing girly more often. We kept picking until there wasn't much left. The fits had gotten more unpredictable, so Parker countered them with heavier drinking. He'd mix up a thirty-two ounce tumbler of Beam and Sprite and head out to the garage at night. Say he was working. Kept a dorm fridge of High Life out there, too. He'd fluff up the recycling container by the fridge with the cereal boxes and newspapers and junk mail on top, and shove his crushed empties under it all. I'd sit in the living room just a wall away, listening to all the clatter. He didn't think I could hear him trying to cover his tracks, but I could.

We hardly touched by then. Even after he got a handle on the drinking, and even once he started going to the meetings, the fits carried on. I never got better at handling them. I tried to read when they were coming on, but I never could. They averaged about one every six weeks over these past three years. Maybe I could've asked more questions, but maybe he could have told me more, too. Instead it just all rotted right there in front of us. It's like we stood there frozen, just watching a love slowly die. A beast once nurtured, steadily becoming motionless. The TV went on and on. It supplied a kind of static undercurrent. It was like a soundtrack for our denial. Suze Orman or Golden Girls or QVC. I'd lay there covered up in a blanket and Parker would pass through the room. Heading out. Coming back late. That TV drone became my company, and those days I made sure to keep it going. God knows when company's droning on and on, you can dance around the quiet spaces that make you have to talk about things. So that's the way we kept it.

The drinking was all the sneaking I could figure. I never found anything else suspicious. No perfume smells or earrings in the floorboard or suspicious hairs on the car seats. No strange calls in the night. But it's hard to know. Especially once the mind goes there, picturing him seeing someone. With Parker it was always Shane this, and Leon that. It probably was only Shane and Leon. Maybe some of the other guys from work, too. But damn if my mind hadn't already gone there, and I found once it does it usually stays in some way or another. I only felt more and more like shit about everything I ever was, and everything I'd come to be.

I called and told Maureen I felt like I was really undone. Finally coming apart. I was gaining weight and sleeping strange, and just driving around some nights smoking cigarette after cigarette. I bought stuff I didn't need, and ate when I wasn't hungry. I'd sit in parking lots for long stretches of time. Head out near sunset and just find a place to be. I'd come home at lunch and get in bed. I was closing off from my own mama and daddy and uncle Jerris and the few friends I'd made in town. And more than anything I worried about Ben. He'd hole up in his room just reading. I couldn't blame him. He was like an islander hunkered down, waiting for a storm to pass over or just dissolve. I was closing off from him, and not sure how to tell him. Not even sure what to tell him. In my mind it was like being in a two-year long silent film. One where a bulldozer circled the house like a shark, slowly taking our whole world apart. Piece by piece and day by day. And all the while none of us inside could hardly move or even talk.

Parker

Back then, Dr. A said it's not Tourette. He said I couldn't develop that this late in life.

Dr. A sure was young and cocky, and he never smiled.

Then Dr. A. said he'd never had a patient like me.

Then Dr. A said first try a diet and exercise change.

He asked all cocky, what's it like when it all goes down?

I said they were blackouts to me.

Dr. A said hmmm.

I said from what I was told, I was unpredictable. That I just said all kinds of strange things. Usually rhymes. Apparently I was pretty loud. With the rhymes, that is.

Dr. A said hmmm.

I was told it was uncomfortable for everyone around me. Episodes. That's what Melinda called them.

Dr. A said hmmm again, all cocky.

I told Dr. A that was all I remembered from the blackouts.

Dr. A said hmmm. Like he knew.

I told Dr. A how it was affecting my life at home and at work.

Dr. A said hmmm, even cockier now.

Dr. A pushed his glasses up his nose and looked at me.

I said so what could it be?

Dr. A. didn't say anything about what it could be. Instead Dr. A said I may be able to contact a behavioral specialist in Memphis. Then he looked back down and wrote some things on some of his stationary.

He said I might not need medicine, but rather a psychologist.

Then he said if it wasn't a psychologist I needed, it might be behavioral medicine.

I said What's the difference between seeing a behavioral specialist and going the route of behavioral medicine? Should I do both?

He gave the piece of paper to me and his phone rang. He answered it and yelled Hey, Jules! Then he cut out of the room. That's the last I saw of Dr. A.

I went out to the car and put Dr. A's paper in the glove box. It stayed buried in there under the operator's manual and insurance papers and fast food coupons, and Melinda didn't ever know about that visit.

And then I drank about all I could.

Every day.

For a little over two years.

So I'm told.

I don't remember much of it.

I was just renting a feeling.

Not much else.

Back then I'd drink almost anywhere except in front of her. Just to try and keep calm. Just to hold it all off. I'd drink with friends, alone, in cars, in movie theaters, in the work van, on top of the work van, in the warehouse, in the garage, in the yard, on the back patio, in the shower, at breakfast if she was gone, as I was making breakfast if she was gone, in the rain, in the sun, in fields, in hotel bars, in hotel rooms, in hotel hallways, in elevators, in ditches, on back roads, and in church. I came to drink big in church. During church. Wine. They had it all over the place. The Spring pancake supper had reached full capacity. Seemed like everyone from the whole congregation was gathered in the banquet room, just off the sanctuary. It started to get so loud in there, just a din of small talk and more and more faces in my face. I felt my breath starting to move fast and moved toward the door. Maybe a fit. I caught a break in the conversation and Melinda was talking to Deacon Baker's wife, Carnie. When the coast was clear I snuck down to the kitchen. I got into the lower pantry cabinets where I knew all the wine was stored. I'd been there a few times before. I found one of the twist offs and took a big enough gulp toward comfort. To keep a fit away. Most of my torso was in the cabinet. I drank fast and my legs stuck out of the doors, extending onto the floor beyond me. A door slammed off to my left. I twisted the cap back on the wine fast, then wormed myself out of the pantry. I was still on the floor and there wasn't time enough to stand up and act like none of this was happening. I got myself out of the cabinet and sat up. I turned toward the left and in walked Deacon Baker. I leaned back against the cabinet, feeling the first pangs of the buzz I'd fought so hard for. I felt the wet of wine on my collar and tried to straighten myself up.

Parker?

Hey, Mr. Baker.

Deacon—

Sure. Deacon.

Deacon Baker is the full story. You know that.

Sure, I know—

What are you doing here?

I was just—

No, wait. Before you go on. I'll come on down to you, he said.

He slowly started to sit on the floor.

No, Deacon, I'll—

No, Parker, I insist. Let me sit down next to you here.

In that time, he sat down, cross-legged. He was in a black suit and all the fabric and the gross length of his red tie sprawled under and around him. Dressy for a pancake supper, I thought. His white hair was combed hard left, and his steel grey eyes never moved away from mine.

But Deacon—

No, Parker. It's no problem. I've got time.

Time for what, Deacon?

Let's just say I'm here to listen, he said, grinning.

Right then Melinda walked in. She said Hon, I've been looking for you. Then she said Hon, it's time to go, and pulled me up off the floor. She pulled me toward the door from the kitchen that led out to the parking lot. I looked back and Deacon Baker didn't get up. He just sat there motionless in the floor, still cross-legged, with his eyes still fixed on me as we left. He was grinning, still at the ready to listen.

Three weeks later the Easter sermon ran long. I told Melinda I was going to the restroom real quick, then ducked out the back of the sanctuary and took the stairs down to the kitchen pantry. I got down on all fours and looked through the cabinets, but all the wine was gone. I looked through the other lower cabinets, and then started to open all the cupboard doors. Nothing. I could hear the start of the benediction above me. There was usually the benediction, a small song, then a pass-the-peace kind of farewell amongst everyone, so I knew I still had a little time.

I went into the ladies room just off the kitchen and released two palmfuls of hand sanitizer into my hands. I took a breath and slammed my face into the gel. I inhaled and sucked whatever I could down and tried not to throw up. My own private communion. I hated it, and in a minute's time I gulped every bit of it down. I went into a stall, took a stream of toilet paper and wiped away all the excess. I rinsed my face and fumbled my way back upstairs to catch Pastor Ross's parting words. The buzz was coming on pretty quick, and my mouth was still gelatinous and unpleasant. I took a deep breath, and with my new buzz the world started to ease some. I leaned against the back wall. I could hear folks asking if Melinda and Ben and me would make it to Easter lunch at Hallahan's when Deacon Baker walked over.

Parker, my friend.

Heyyy, Deac—

One of the strongest of our flock here. How are you?

I'm . . . I'm all right.

I could feel my blood slowing, surrendering to the grip of all the alcohol. The base of my skull felt heavier, my shoulders relaxed, and I was cradled in some deep comfort long sought.

Will you all be joining us for fellowship lunch today?

Ahhh, I don't—

We probably won't be, Melinda said cutting me off.

Prob'ly not today, Deacon, I said. I was slurring some now.

Oh, well that's too—

It is too bad, but it's just not a good time for us today, Melinda said, clutching my right arm.

I fumbled the keys out of my front right pocket and handed them over to her. It was a long and sloppy move. She took my right hand, and her and Ben and me all stepped toward the side door under the purple, red, and yellow stained glass image of St. Paul. The noon sun was high in the sky now. The summer bugs sang and a low breeze swept in through the front door of the church. We stepped into the humid, bright pain of the afternoon, shuffled down the steps and headed to the car across the street.

Melinda

Back when Parker and I were new, back when I was still at The Lantern, we'd steal away to Tunica for a weekend. I made pretty good money tending bar and would save up here and there. We kept a big plastic Folgers coffee can on top of the fridge, and I'd throw maybe ten or twenty bucks in it once every couple weeks. Sometimes more on holidays or NFL playoff weekends if I won some money in the bar betting pool. We'd call and book a room at Isle Of Capri or maybe Hollywood Station, and head out. We'd listen to that Tom Petty Wildflowers CD on the drive and sometimes we'd even take a mind to pull off and make out on a side road. The reds and oranges of a sunset would sprawl over the Arkansas sky, and Parker would drive with his hand on my leg. One thing that really sticks out from those drives is that whole outro of It's Good To Be King. It fit the surroundings just right to me and I can still hear it and smell the smells of the cotton and soybean fields. The sigh of another day gone by in our little world. We'd arrive after dark and valet the car because it was free and made us feel important. We'd settle in for a weekend of buffets and slots and cheap drinks and not many worries further than when or what to eat. Everything we needed was under one roof, and we could just leave the car parked. There was a spot out back of the hotel where we'd take a couple of poolside chairs further out in the grass, on toward the levee. If it was a clear night we'd sit and watch the sunset over the Mississippi. We'd stock a cooler full of Bud Lights and candy bars and orange juice and whatever else and bring it up the stairwell, keep it in the room. It always felt good to have freshies on hand and it felt good to save a few bucks. Most times we made love right when we got to the room. Then we'd shower up and roam around the rest of the night through a sea of blips and blinks and bright lights. Sipping on beers, eyes wide open in a world draped in neon. Everything aglow in pinks and yellows and reds and blues. It was like an amusement park for us grown-ups. We'd stay up and watch hotel cable. We'd laugh quietly at the taps of the bedposts on the other side of the wall. The hallway moans of others. Gamblers and cheaters and old lovers reunited. I was better back then. Parker was, too. When we were good, we were really good. Love had a different shape back then. God, we fucked like kids.

Parker

It's probably the tics, Dr. B said.

What?

The tics. Just random movements. Vocalizations, he said, looking over my file.

The way you've described the fits, it may be a complex version, but I think you should ride it out for a while.

Ride it out? I asked.

Yeah, just watch your diet and exercise. Go easy on the caffeine.

I do all that. Mostly.

This may be due to an abnormality within the brain, or depression, or stress.

Depression?

Or all three, he said.

I paused.

Of course it could be ADHD, too. All of these things could be late-onset.

Suddenly Dr. B was cocky, too.

What I'm saying is go easy, he said.

Easy?

How many hours a week are you clocking?

I don't know. Somewhere between 45 and 55.

See about peeling that back some.

How? I need to make money.

Meditate.

Meditate?

Go easy, he said. I know you've probably thought this out but if you're in a public space and you feel one coming on, try and get yourself somewhere quiet. Maybe a backyard or a bathroom. Even the car.

All right, but—

But overall, just go easy. And come see me again in three months.

So no prescription, I said?

Cut your hours back, exercise, and meditate, he said. That's the prescription. He headed out the door toward another call. Suddenly full cocky, now.

I went on home and shut all the blinds. I took off my shirt and sat cross-legged in the middle of the living room. I put my hands facing upward on my knees and took a few deep breaths. At first I felt silly, but this was like I'd seen on TV and in the movies. After maybe three minutes of deep breaths I started to feel pretty good. I kept my eyes closed and kept taking deep breaths. I started thinking on this new setup, with Melinda and me living apart. For once I didn't think about it in an angry way. Just thinking about our new paths some, and how Ben might be handling it. He was a young man suddenly. He was at the age where he was starting to say thank you. He would say it with a straight face, holding eye contact so that I knew he meant it. Maybe the recent setbacks in our lives brought on more compassion. Struggle and loss can do that.

Thank you for doing the laundry.

Thank you for handing me the knife.

Thank you for the supper.

Thank you for the ride back to Mama's.

He was more focused. He'd eased into a more sincere way of talking. He knew himself better. He was growing up.

The summer days were young, but it was already hot. The regular sound of lawnmowers or weed eaters hummed through the neighborhood nearly every morning. The fireflies were back, the dogwoods still thriving, and the air weighed heavy in the afternoons. Melinda had left almost five months ago. She'd moved twenty-five minutes up the road to Clarkton. Her sister had two extra rooms for her and Ben. Melinda had also taken up with a new guy. Coached Little League in his spare time. Rotary or Kiwanis, maybe. His name was Chad, I heard. Intense and fit and caring, I heard. Served in Afghanistan or Iraq and was a good cook, I heard. So it all was said.

I was still in the house. It was a lot more space than I needed but I'd stay a while longer. Work with the cable company was busy, and I had a little money saved back. I needed some more furniture, and maybe some better decorations. Melinda took a lot of that stuff — the stuff that makes a house a home. She either put it in storage for wherever she was going next, or boxed it up and put it out in Maureen's garage. Ben switched schools to Clarkton when Melinda moved, and stayed with me every other weekend. I didn't have a lot to offer around here. I could admit that with certainty. I've never been much of a cook, and there's only a few small things even in the fridge. We kept his bed here for now. I slept on a mattress and a box spring in Melinda's and my old room. I'd found some new curtains for cheap and, little by little, was trying to make something of the place. Looking at it all I think Ben felt for both me and his mama. Last year's attitude had been replaced by this new thoughtfulness. I was thankful for that.

I opened my eyes and felt a little better. I took one more deep breath and stretched my arms upwards. I stood up, put my shirt back on and laid down on the couch under the cool breeze of the fan for a little while until I dozed off.

The next day was Saturday. I sat at the kitchen table paying bills and heard the low buzz of the mower outside. Ben had gotten up before me and was already cutting the grass. I had a good view of the backyard from the table. He came in sweaty.

You did a diagonal cut and not a straight one, I said, looking up from the bills and checkbook.

Yeah, he said breathing heavy.

It looks good.

Ben looked back out at the yard and shrugged.

You can tell a lot about a person by the way they cut their grass, he said.

Well, it looks good.

Thanks.

You mowed around the rain lilies.

Yeah.

No one's hardly ever spared the rain lilies around here when they mow.

Well, that's the kind of person I want to be, he said.

He went on down the hall to shower, but then turned back and stopped at the edge of the hallway.

Dad?

Yeah, son.

I was wondering when I might be able to have a car of my own.

I don't know, Ben. I'll have to think about that some.

Ok. Like . . .

Like what?

Like, for how long? Like, how long will you have to think about it?

You keep sparing the rain lilies and the like and it'll be here sooner than later, I said.

He smiled and gave a small nod, then went on down the hall.

We went to the Brown Derby for our traditional Saturday burgers. Our town considered it a bar, and they usually wouldn't let a kid his age in, but for two years now they'd made exceptions. Ben could almost pass for being of-age anyway. We took our regular booth and settled in. There were a few guys shooting pool and the same baseball game was on both TVs.

I haven't asked in a while, but how's Clarkton?

It's fine, he said, hesitant.

What do you think about the school situation?

A little behind what we were doing here, but it's fine.

You think Mama's gonna hang at Maureen's for a while or get her own place?

I don't know. It's a place to land.

Is it a good place to land? I asked.

It's cheap, Ben said.

And mama doesn't seem to wanna move me again. At least not right now.

For all the things that Melinda and I had come to disagree on, we both at least agreed on that. We didn't want Ben juggled around any more than he already was.

Girl? I asked.

What?

You got a girl up there yet?

He turned away and looked over at the pool table, then back.

Well? I laughed.

Couple wrote me notes some when school was in. They call sometime.

Yeah?

It's nothin', dad. He looked back at the pool table.

What about friends?

A couple, I guess. Here and there.

You gonna work this summer?

Maybe. Maybe pitch watermelons if I can get rides out to the fields.

A teenage kid brought our burgers out and we ate. Pool balls clacked behind us and the announcer's voice on the TV escalated like someone had scored or made a good play.

How is your mama? I asked, but as soon as the words were out of my mouth I realized I only half cared to know.

She's all right, he chewed.

Working some at the farm bureau, doing books. Part time.
Summer job?
I don't know. I guess. She seems to like it ok.
We went on eating. The teenage kid came around and asked if everything was okay right when both our mouths were full. Without looking up Ben and I both nodded yes.

Melinda had moved from job to job in her last couple of years here, from the funeral home to the savings and loan, then to the steakhouse and the pizza place. She and a cook she'd been sweet on were closing up, but had forgotten to lock the door. One of the other cooks came by to pick up his check and found her leaned up against the ice machine with her skirt up, the first cook on top of her. They were both fired the next day and the whole town got to talking. Then word got around that people had already seen her out with the Iraq vet guy. There wasn't much to fight about. It happened. Some folks get frisky and something takes over and before you know it you're propped up on an ice machine and it's all happening. With a lot of folks I'd guess it's hard to know when the switch might flip to where it's time to risk it all. That night told me that Melinda had long moved on mentally, and now physically. She moved up to Clarkton a week or so after the ice machine thing. New town. Clean slate.

Melinda

Maureen said all the right things.
　　At least all the things I wanted to hear.
　　Mama'd been gone a few years now.
　　Dad might as well have been.
　　Hadn't seen him in four.
　　Fallen worse for the drinking.
　　Up in Rolla.
　　Or somewhere near there.
　　Never once laid a hand on us.
　　But the words he said.
　　You girls'll never amount to shit.
　　Mama ain't in charge here.
　　I am.
　　You heard me.
　　All slurred.
　　So many nights.
　　The yelling with mama.
　　Late when he thought we were asleep.
　　Word got around about him.
　　Maureen said she had space for me.

She said just come on, girl.
She said we'll stay up, girl.
She said we'll get your room together.
She said we'll make it all your own, girl.
She said you don't need him no more, girl.
She said I can't blame you, girl.
She said no one in their right mind would, girl.
She said Ben can come on too, girl.
She said he'll have his own room and we'll stay up girl.
She said I'll take you around town, girl.
She said I know a guy named Chad.
She said he's single.
She said he's fine.
She said I'll introduce y'all.
She hawed and was sure of herself.
She was confident all the way.
She said I got you, girl.
She said come on, girl.
Maureen pushed hard.
Maureen always pushed hard.
I said my son comes first.
I said if he's okay with it, we'll come.
I sure hope he's okay with it.

Melinda

I still can't hear It's Good To Be King.

I act strong.

Some days I actually am strong.

But some days I still see those drives with Parker.

I left a buggy full of groceries in the bread aisle at Kroger a few months ago.

I left it there when that song came on the grocery store sound system.

I went straight out front. Sat on a bench.

I lit a cigarette and figured that might buy enough time 'til it was over.

I looked across the cracked asphalt in all the sunlight and the heat.

Families together, running their errands.

Couples, too.

I smoked and put my arms straight down at my sides.

I smoked a little more.

Shawna Myers walked by with her little boy Henry at her side. They said hi.

I smiled a fake smile and without saying anything, took my last drag.

I put the cigarette out on the sole of my boot.

I got up off the bench and pitched it in the trash.

Then I went back on in to my buggy, still waiting there on the bread aisle.

Parker

Sir, can I start with you?
  Yeah, I think I'm read—
  Great, I can get back to you if someone else wants to start, he motioned to the other side of the table.

Terror Train!

Excuse—? the server said, turning back to me.

Black Sunday!
  Ain't no Jimmy Carter!
  You ain't Superfly Snuka!

(Shove table, kick legs. Fork slam and water spill.)

Apparently that's some of what I said.

At least that's what Melinda said I said.

A lot of people saw.

I didn't have the right kind of insurance for this kind of thing. Not with the cable company. The first two visits were out of pocket. I spent an hour on the phone with the rep from PatriotCare. She said it was too ambiguous a thing for my policy. I couldn't get a straight answer out of McCarran, my boss, other than he said he'd continue to check back in on it. Was it preexisting? he asked. I think so, I said. He said he'd look into it. But I don't think he did. Time came for a third opinion, and I was at my end. To his credit, McCarran loaned me some money to go. Not for a prescription. Just for another assessment.

We need you back full time, he said.

This is for both of us, he said.

I drove down to Memphis to see Dr. C., the behavioral specialist Dr. A talked about some time back. After hearing me out, he looked over my file, which had been sent down from Dr. B.

It's definitely the tics, Dr. C said.

The tics?

Just a nervous reaction. From the way you've described this to me, I think we're dealing with phonic tics.

What does that mean?

It's a simple nervous reaction due to your present chemical makeup. We're going to work to keep that at bay. I know you've had the outbursts, but has anything violent happened?

No. But I suspect it could.

We're gonna try a round of Clonidine, he said. Let's try a three-month dose and see if that quells them.

Why didn't the first two doctors I saw prescribe anything? I asked.

Lazy. Or wrong, Dr. C said.

Or both, he added, snapping the folder shut.

I picked up my first round at the Walgreen's on Summer Avenue. The whole trip took all the money that McCarran had loaned me, and I had to put another hundred and thirty-three on my credit card. I walked out to the parking lot, despondent. Flattened by some so-called healthcare system that had always been a mystery to me. I unpacked my prescription and started the car. I looked over at the box of Clonidine on the passenger seat. I went ahead and took my first dosage before I pulled out of the parking lot onto Summer Avenue. I found I-30 Westbound and crossed the new bridge into Arkansas, then West Memphis. I turned north on I-55 and pulled off at a liquor store in Marion. I went on in and picked up some beer. I got back into the car and watched all the cars speeding north and south on 55. Late afternoon had set in, and two old hounds frolicked off in the grass separating the parking lot and the field next to the liquor store. Strays. I pulled two cold sixteen-ounce Budweisers from the paper bag sitting shotgun and drained both of them in a matter of five or six minutes. I turned the engine over, got back on I-55, and drove on north. The sun was peeking in and out of the clouds to the left of me, and I felt almost normal by the Missouri state line.

Rachel

I'd saved like hell working at the country club back then. Old white men everywhere, telling me this and that. Swoll up prostates and equally swoll opinions on everything, it seemed. Flirting and wanting seats by the window and asking for extra half and half and lemons just for an excuse to talk. I was a third their age. My daddy hated it and wanted details on who all did or said what. I think he hated those old men. Talked about flattening the tires of their Cadillacs and Lexuses out front. I kept my head down and kept saving. I kept on with daddy that those old men were harmless. And they were. They'd tip well and their wives would always take their keys and walk them out, teetering and tipsy. I socked away the money and went up to beauty school in Cape Girardeau. I took the jokes I heard about beauty school in stride, but I was in motion at least, unlike a lot of folks here in Rutherford.

Try this, girl. Try that, girl. You look amaaaaazing, girl. Oh, that won't work, girl. Too light. Too dark. Not that Revlon stuff. Not that ColorStay, girl. Something better. Here. This. We should go out after, girl. Cheddar's. Or Chili's. It's Friday! It's Hump Day! Thursday's the new Friday! Long weekend! To a tough Monday! To Spring Break! It's almost the holidays! The holidays are over! It don't matter. So long as there's drinks, girl. That, with all of them, for more than three years. For the most part that beauty school was a framework of gossip and envy built on a foundation of fakeness. A pontoon of desperation floating on a pond of vodka, and you've mostly got it.

I did find one friend up there. Janelle. She was from up in Hannibal and took me in as a roommate for a while. The drinks with her every night became as rhythmic and predictable as the evening news. It was just understood that that's what we'd do. Either with girls from school, or without. At a bar or on the porch. It never mattered. Even after I got my own apartment Janelle and I got together. She was about the only one I could trust from school. She actually looked me in the eye when we talked, and like me, she wanted to keep away from the dirt and shop talk. She'd wanted out of Hannibal just like I'd wanted out of Rutherford, and beauty school was her portal just like it was mine.

I dated a Kia salesman there for a while. David Stockton. He came from money, but still kept the job at the dealership to try and prove something to himself and to his family. He'd had dad issues and needed to follow through. It was the first time I'd been around someone who didn't have to think much about money. His paychecks and commissions were play money. He belonged to the country club up there and would take me around. I saw the same old rich men there that I did back home. Talking about their same rich people problems. The left rear tire in my Corvette has a slow leak. This Ping nine-iron is shit. The valet service is terrible. David would laugh it all off, and that made him seem real to me. He tried at his job at the dealership and didn't take it for granted. He bought me clothes and would take me on weekend trips to St. Louis. We'd stay at the Sheraton Westport and eat at upscale restaurants for a couple of days. That's when I started dressing nice. I wanted to look like I came from money, too. And as soon as it felt like something, it was nothing. David moved on with Kim from accounting at the dealership, and none of it surprised me all that much. Kim from accounting dressed nice. But I dressed nicer. Still do. Almost every day.

But that new loneliness led to more drinks, either with Janelle or not. It led to my leaving beauty school early, and Cape, too. That all brought me back to Rutherford, and to these meetings eventually.

Maureen

Sure glad to have Melinda here.

And Ben.

I don't know every detail.

At least not yet.

But it was hard to get a handle on Parker anymore.

Seemed loving but not loveable.

Or maybe the reverse.

Either way, lotta maintenance.

Melinda said she's got Ben to think about, and I said okay.

Melinda said he'll be with his Daddy on the weekends, and I said okay.

Melinda said are you mad at me because I cheated?

I said hell, no.

Melinda didn't say much about Parker's fits anymore.

Not her problem anymore.

Melinda said Parker's drinking was under control.

Still not her problem anymore.

I cut out at lunch that Friday and went home to get their rooms ready.

We'll be tight, but it's Melinda.

And Ben.

He's so sweet from what I know.

Should be no trouble.

One room was a storeroom catch-all basically, but I'd make it work.

The cats had had their way in there and it all needed to be cleaned good, but I'd make it work. I'd do anything for her.

Parker could go figure for himself.

My take is that he'd needed to figure for himself for a long time.

Chad would come around some now anyway.

Be a man figure, checkin' in on us.

Melinda and him had already gone out a couple times.

Maybe he'd cook for us now and then.

Maybe he could fix some things around here.

But Melinda I'd do anything for.

Bring it on, girl.

I got the wine ready and iced and the back porch chairs and table dusted off.

Stack of DVDs laid out for Ben on the coffee table.

He likes Gunsmoke and Archie Bunker, I hope.

Hot Pockets in the freezer.

We could order pizza and maybe a good sunset would come about that first night.

Get us a nice buzz on.

Have a time.

Parker

The pool balls clacked again and I asked Ben what he'd been up to in his free time other than the jobs.

Working out and reading some. Stephen King, mostly.

I'm thinking about basketball tryouts in the Fall. May be a long shot, but at a smaller school like Clarkton, who knows, he said looking back off at the TV.

You made any new friends? I asked.

Couple guys. Carl and Danny. Danny's got a car and we ride around sometimes. Up to Poplar Bluff even, one time.

Are they all right?

They're all right I guess. Still trying to figure them at certain points.

How?

Not sure how much to tell you.

Go on, I said.

I don't know. They run a little fast, he said stirring his straw in his soda.

How?

Carl broke out a little weed on a ride last week.

Really?

Yeah. I didn't know he had it 'til he lit up.

You try any?

Ben paused and stirred the straw more. Yeah. A little, he said.

Now are you mad?

No.

Was it really just a little?

Yeah, it wasn't but one of those one-hitter things.

Well, did you like it?

Not really. I coughed real bad. Didn't feel too good after.

You sure you're not mad.

No. I'm not mad.

It made me feel real paranoid, he said.

Then it must've been all right, I said.

I don't wanna mess with it again I don't think.

Ben wadded up his napkin and put it in the basket, then looked back off at the TV. He looked back at me.

Really? You're really not mad?

Son, you've seen me at my worst. And not that long ago. You loved me through that, right?

Yeah.

I'm not mad. I've done a lot of things that didn't make much sense, but to be mad at you for something like that wouldn't make any at all.

Okay.

Who was driving?

Danny.

Was Danny smoking weed, too?

No.

All right, then. But you do remember it's illegal.

Yeah.

And if you're thinking about basketball, you gotta—

I know. he said.

I could tell he was ready to move on by now. These windows were short sometimes.

I just wanna say a couple more things, but I want you to look at me and not the TV.

What's that?

Trying all these new things is part of being young. Most every kid does it at some point. I just want you to remember to respect yourself and those around you. You find yourself wanting to get a little buzz on, look at the ceiling once in a while.

What do you mean?

Ceiling starts to spin, it's time to call it. Anything beyond that is gonna be bad. Sometimes real bad.

Why? he asked.

Just take note of who you're with. I'm only with you half the time, but I'll come get you any time, all the time. Understand?

Okay, he said and looked back at the TV.

A lot of this stuff is in our blood, I said. But I need you to look right back at me and tell me you won't drive after messing with any of it.

I won't.

I raised my hand up over the baskets in an arm wrestling position.

Promise?

He raised his hand up and gripped mine.

Promise.

We got out of our seats. I reached in my pocket and found a wrinkled twenty to cover our bill, and then I hugged him strong.

We settled up and walked out to the car. I had to get him back up to Clarkton, and we had about fifteen minutes before we needed to hit the road. He asked again about when he might be able to have a car of his own, and I said I'd need to think about that.

He said he'd been saving and would try to meet me in the middle with it.

He didn't know it but I had a line on a little used Nissan Frontier at McGee's across town. It had been used as a farm truck over in Pemiscot County for years and had about 132,000 miles on it. I was set to pick it up on Monday morning but I wanted it to be a surprise for him in a couple weeks when he came back. I'd saved a while, and his behavior had sure been good over these recent months. I thought it was time and I thought he had earned it. He was becoming more independent. Melinda was gone and soon Ben would be out there driving around on his own. I'd miss taking him places, but my heart thumped when I thought about giving him the truck.

I asked if he thought he was responsible enough to take care of a car.

He said he was, and I knew he was.

He said he didn't want to have to bug his mama and me and his friends for rides everywhere.

He said he liked the idea of being able to drive to school, and then down to see me on his own before long.

I said I liked that, too.

Ben

Mama's so down.
So quiet.
She doesn't talk about it much.
But I can tell.
Mama forces out smiles when she doesn't wanna smile.
Mama laughs with Maureen when she doesn't always wanna laugh.
Polite smile here.
Forced laugh there.
Must feel like work.
Lotta energy to keep doing that.
Three of us hanging around here.
Sometimes four.
Chad.
Hangs around some when Mama and Maureen are at work.
Maybe a little too much.
Man figure, I guess.
Fix a porch light, I guess.
Jump a dead battery or clean a gutter, I guess.
Mama likes him, I guess.

Or liked him.
Chad's got time.
At a life crossroads, Chad says.
Gonna do somethin' new soon, Chad says.
Gonna diversify and collaborate, Chad says.
Gonna keep it real, Chad says.
Definitely by Fall, Chad says.
Take it to the next level, Chad says.
What you readin', kid? Chad says.
I say Stephen King.
Clancy, Chad says.
What?
Tom Clancy. Chad says.
Cool, I say.
It's tight here some days.
So I walk a lot.
I say I'm gonna go get some air.
I say I'm gonna go to the store.
Streets and sidewalks and alleys.
I know Clarkton all right now.
Some rough kids around here.
Some drink hard already.
I don't want to.
Not after seeing dad and what he went through.
I love him so much.
But dad was bad.
Smoked just that once.
With Carl and Danny.
Everything spun a little.
Dad was right.
Had to call it.
Tryin' to be good.
If not for myself, then at least for mama.

Parker

It sounds like a bad situation but I'd have to look at it, Tony said.

What do you mean?

Well, I'd have to look but the way you're describing the transmission sounds, seems like it might be on the brink.

Like it needs to be replaced?

Probably. From the sound your describing. It's not cheap, but you know who does good work is Pendleton's.

Pendleton's?

Yeah, I've used 'em for years and they're four generations in now.

What's a transmission gonna run you think?

Mmm, probably two or three thousand, Tony grimaced.

Two—

But you could maybe score one used for a thousand or so. Maybe less. Anyway, what else you say you need today?

Air filters. Both engine and cabin, I staggered.

Oh, okay. Well, they're over here on this aisle. These Fram ones are good. The Extra Guards are fine but for a little more money these Ultra Premiums are good. With these you got—

No YOU got that I got nothin'
What, Park-?
I said YOU got the air filters, me I got old pants see my old pants?
Parker?
Old, old pants! You cannibal boy?
Park—
Ima get away from the cannibal boy! Get away get away!
Air filter, hair filter, bye!

I came to, sitting on the curb out front of the store. I looked over and Tony and Max, the store manager, leaned out the sliding glass doors looking at me. Like a zoo animal or a rabid dog they were afraid to come near. I looked back forward. The traffic sped by and the breeze picked up.

We stopped at the Dollar General before leaving for Clarkton. I needed nine-volts, ketchup, bread, and those tallboys of Arnold Palmer iced tea/lemonade had been on sale two-for-one the last time I was there. We walked in from the heat and the A/C made the air feel thinner. It was relentlessly bright outside, and our eyes adjusted to the inside light. We were whiplashed into a den of offshore, manufactured stacks and stock. We saw the rows of candy and napkins and paper plates and sodas and beer. A guy was hanging up swimsuits and T-shirts and stacking beach towels and colored see-thru plastic cups on the seasonal items row. The lady said Welcome to Dollar General, and for a minute I got dizzy. I faded into all the clothes and flip flops and glare and rubbery smells of the place. For a minute I thought of how many of these Dollar Generals there were in the world. I felt like we could have been anywhere. Rutherford could have been anywhere. Ben went off toward the drink coolers. I stopped and looked over the trial-size toiletries and bathroom items. I thought about how Melinda and I used to stop here and buy last odds and ends before we left town for Tunica or Markham Springs or wherever. How far away that life seemed now. Ben rounded the corner with a bag of Bugles and an orange Gatorade. I floundered back into the present and picked out the things I needed for home. We got in line and Ben wondered aloud if folks from Wellington Addition shopped here. I said the folks from Wellington Addition might, but probably don't talk about it.

I got Ben back up to Maureen's place in time. Now that he was almost grown I didn't have to go to the door anymore. Just a far, cold wave from the steering wheel. I'd watch him in the house, then pull away. I called Rachel on the drive back. It'd been a few days now. I met her at the edge of the Wal-Mart parking lot. She looked great. Her red hair was curled, and it looked great. She wore a sensible black skirt and a cream-colored blouse. Probably just off her shift at Hillen's, a department store downtown where she'd worked the makeup counter for a couple months now. I was still trying to understand her life. I was still trying to understand so many things about her. From here in town, but how'd we miss each other for so long? In Rutherford? How'd we not know? Daddy, long disappeared. Unpredictable mama she said, but I'd never met her. Two brothers, long moved away to Tennessee. That's about all I knew.

She didn't say a word.

She just got in the car and crawled across the front seat.

She wrapped her legs around me.

She said honey.

She said baby.

She held my head in her hands.

She kissed my forehead, then down to my lips.

I tasted her lipstick.

She said it's been days.

She looked out the windshield, then out the back.

Then over both shoulders.

She said let's get in the back seat.

She said now.

And we did.

She stopped and said let me look at you.

She rubbed my face and neck.

She climbed on top.

Grabbed hold of my hands and forced them around to her ass. Her skirt raising up some as she pressed forward.

She said there.

She said that's it, hon.

She leaned into me.

She smelled like a day's work, and I'm guessing I smelled like county-wide regret. Perfume and menthols. Slight smell of decayed sweat as she closed in and unbuttoned my work shirt. I wrapped my legs right back around her. We kissed long and her tongue ran across my neck. I held her tight in the heat of the back seat. All an oven, now. No one seeing as far as I could tell. She untucked me, and then her. Grabbed hold of my left hand and shoved it under her blouse. She unbuttoned me, then her. The seat vinyl stuck to us and tried not to let go any time we moved one way or another. Squeaks and buckles underneath. Her lips on my forehead again. My hands back down on her strong hips, pressing forward. It'd been days. We didn't care if anyone saw. Right then caring was for other people to worry about.

Rachel

I met him at my second meeting. Methodist church basement on Tuesday nights. He'd been in and out of there for a while, he said to all of us during the introductions that night. Long battle, doctors, occasional episodes he didn't want to get into explaining, he said. Drinking was how he tempered it, he said. He leaned up in his chair, elbows on his knees, looking down and listening to everyone else's stories. His jeans were worn at the thighs, and he wore weathered brown work boots. He had on what looked like a knockoff Izod golf shirt. The kind of thing to where he wanted to look nice for these things, but that he also looked out of place in.

I got up, straightened my skirt and went over to where the coffee was, just for an excuse to see him from another angle.

Hi, I'm Brandon.

Hi, Brandon, they'd say.

And Brandon would go on and on and how his wife this, and his third DUI that.

I stood there and stirred my coffee.

Hi, I'm Larissa.

Hi, Larissa, they'd say.

After that all the sounds became one, and my tunnel vision for Parker started to dagger through all the voices. The back of his neck was worn with the kind of permanent wrinkles that a life in hard outdoor labor brings on. I went back to my seat and he was still hunched, elbows to knees and apparently deep in thought, but by now his left leg was bouncing up and down. Really twitching. His nose and middle face were sunburned and when he straightened back up at the end of Larissa's story, he looked up at the ceiling. He had tears in his eyes and he mostly looked like he'd been hit by a truck. His leg stopped twitching right around then and he looked straight over at me. Through me, it felt like.

The town's so small I'm guessing he knew a few people in the room. Maybe that was it. Maybe that was the source of the nervousness. Just looking at him I could tell it took a lot for him just to show up. Just to get his boots on and come here.

In recent meetings when he talked, he talked about his son. Never said his name, but I could tell he was mostly doing this for his son. Baby steps. A lot of us trying to just pull through a day. Two days. A week. I gave up guessing what he'd been through and anchored all my love for him on the single notion that he'd do this for his boy. Sometimes, sitting there, I'd try to picture him a few years back. Then farther back than that. Good Christ, he looked awful. Beautiful, too.

Maureen

I cleared off the island. Ben was gone, I think down at the park shooting hoops, and Melinda'd gone to the bank and maybe the store. I flipped the TV on to the news, and then Price Is Right so I could watch and fold. More laundry here now but I didn't mind. Ben's shirts were giant. Good grief, I thought, holding one out. How'd all this time passed so fast since he was just a little tyke?

A woman from Detroit bid just a dollar under the real price and everyone else bid over. Big red-haired girl. Came running up on the stage and almost frenched Drew Carey. I swear I saw slobber glistening on his cheek. He gave a half-smile and then they started playing that old game where the little mountaineer climbs upward in his knickers. The one with the yodeling.

I kept folding. A few quarters and what looked like a folded-up note fell out of Ben's Levi's. And where'd Melinda get this black lacy underwear? Goodness. For who? Chad?

It's all right to look, right? Is it all right to look anymore? What with all this political correctness? Chad's cheekbones reminded me of that old football player from the '80s, the one with the weird hair. Bosworth, I think. And when he talks he sounds like Tommy Lee Jones. I felt bad for thinking all this stuff. But, damn.

He told me once, but I can't remember how long he was over there. Kabul or something. And he went on about what he was doing there and I can hardly remember that. Infantry division, I think he said, but I don't know. I wondered what he was like before that. All I know is he came back intense. Lightning blue eyes and strong forearms. When he talked people sure seemed to listen. Some people around town say he's a flat-out hero. Ronnie at the bank sure does. I wonder if he was in the trenches and had to sleep on the ground over there. Up 'til all hours with his eyes set into a gun, just waiting for a movement from afar. I never even asked what he did for fun while he was there, and I guess I should. Can't imagine what he's seen or what he's been through. Seems like he could fix a few things around here. I already know he can cook. Other day Melinda said do you mind if he comes over and hangs out for a while? Of course I didn't. She said do you mind if Chad this, and do you mind if Chad that? Of course I didn't. What's good for Melinda feels good for me these days. I may give it a drink or two, then call and see if he could cut the grass or fix that gutter over the back porch. Seemed like he felt comfortable enough around here. He'd already cooked for us twice and it was wonderful. Ribs and baked beans and scalloped potatoes and spinach salad that first night. Then he went on and made stuffed pork loin and asparagus and roasted red potatoes and a chocolate icebox pie a few nights later. He even went on and brought beer and white wine and even some Beam that second time. He'd knock, but come on in. Hey babes, he'd say as he was squeezing himself through the front door, arms full of grocery bags. Where he got the money for all that, who knows? I thought he'd hang around a little, but it's starting to feel like more than that. I don't mind. He stays over with Melinda sometimes, but I don't mind. My cigarettes been disappearing some, but I don't mind. Of course I'm not gonna say anything, but I also ain't gonna feel bad for enjoying the scenery.

Ben

Wish I could figure Carl and Danny.
   I like riding around.
   They ask me along.
   Couple times now.
   But not sure.
   First time I heard 'em talking a little shit.
   When we were riding around.
   About a girl I think may be all right.
   Jenny, they said.
   Next time we went out we picked up Jenny.
   Out front of her house.
   Carl drove and I rode up front.
   Danny and Jenny in back.
   Carl played a Three Doors Down cd.
   Then he played Slipknot.
   Danny and Jenny talked in the back.
   I looked off past Carl out toward the fields.
   Danny and Jenny sure sat close.
   Danny had his arm around her.
   His hand on her leg.

Carl said what you think, Ben?
I said I don't know.
Carl said your pick, Ben, where you wanna roll?
I said I don't know, wherever's cool.
Dark was falling.
Home for supper soon, probably.
I heard Danny whisper come on, babe to Jenny.
Jenny said no, real soft.
Then Danny said aw, come on, babe.
Jenny said no a little louder, but still trying to be soft. Not make a scene.
I looked back.
Danny had his hand part way up Jenny's jean skirt.
She pushed his hand back down.
Then I turned back front real quick.
Pretending like I didn't see.
Carl said what you think, Ben?
Home for supper, I guess. I better get—
Naw, Ben. Flash Market first.
But I gotta—
See if someone can get us some beers.
All right, I said.
I used mama's polite smile.
It all felt like work.
Then I looked away.
Out at the fields going by.
Worried I'll be late.
Then worried about that weed thing.
Can't tell mama.
Won't tell mama.
Mama's got enough to worry about.
Maureen's sweet to us.
Maureen took us in for I don't know how long.
Maybe indefinite.
I never heard.
But my room's tough.
Smells.
Cat pee and smoke and Glade.

Hole in the closet floor.
I can see the ground some in the daylight.
And hear critters under there in the night.
Two tall boy dressers.
Plastic storage bins stacked up.
Stationary bike with laundry always hanging on it.
Treadmill with laundry always hanging on it.
Stains on the ceiling tiles.
Magazines and clothes stacked up.
One outlet works.
The other two don't.
No lamp.
Overhead light, or darkness.
Mattress on the floor and a few books.
I put an old picture of dad and me fishing, by the bed.
Just for something familiar.
Some comfort.
My small world.
My small choices.
Maureen's sweet.
But this ain't mine.
I can't tell if this is the beginning of something.
Or the end of something else.
Been a little while now.
Wanna cut some more lawns to keep my mind moving
Keep reading to keep my mind moving.
Keep working out to keep my mind moving.
Maybe basketball.
Maybe even my own car.
A little independence.
Mama's so down.
But she keeps on.
She'd do anything for me, I think.
Those forced smiles.
But always a beautiful smile, mama.
I got you, mama.
Maureen's sweet.
But this ain't mine.

This ain't ours, mama, I thought.
Carl drove on.

Ben

Chad's tough.

Chad spends the night, waits 'til mama and Maureen have gone to work, then mostly chills.

Chad got a new Fatboy.

Chad brought it over to Maureen's last week.

I guess it's here to stay.

Says TV's better here.

Says A/C's better here.

Says his roommate's tough to deal with.

Says his roommate's always hanging around.

Chad goes to Rotary sometimes, then mostly chills.

Chad had a cooking job up 'til April.

Chad had his own place. Last year.

Chad coached some Little League. Last year.

Chad likes to kick it.

Chad likes to start slow, then taper.

At least that's what I see when I'm here.

Last week I said Chad, you wanna throw the ball?

Chad said no.

I said why?

Chad said go out there and throw it up in the air, catch it yourself.

I said what?

Chad said throw it up in the air and catch it yourself. It's the same thing.

Chad never turned away from the TV.

Chad ate from a stadium tumbler.

It was filled with white bread chunks and whole milk.

Chad said good luck.

Car racing was on.

Mama was gone.

Maureen was gone.

I went out there.

I couldn't believe it.

I tried what Chad said.

Ball up.

Ball down.

Sucked.

I sat down on the curb and thought about home.

I looked around and thought about Clarkton.

I looked down and thought about dad down there in Rutherford.

Back inside.

Back in the A/C.

Back in the dark.

Dog in fight, fight in dog, Chad says.

Car racing was still on.

Long, tenor fart resonates off new Fatboy.

Fart reverberations all inside the Fatboy.

Chad laughs, hard cackles.

Chad shifts around on new Fatboy.

Throws his arms out and heaves a big sigh.

Back outside.

Mama likes him?

Chad wears shades in the house some days.

Chad's cradling the tumbler of white bread and whole milk.

Chad's finished half of it.

Chad hits pause and gets up from the Fatboy.

Chad takes a break to go whiz.

Chad says Ben do me a solid and bring me a beer.
Chad says Ben do me a solid and turn down the A/C.
Chad says that your dad in that pic you keep by your bed?
Chad says what's he like?
Chad says well maybe I'll meet him one day.
Four o'clock, first beer.
Four twenty, second beer.
Five o'clock, third beer.
Five thirty, fourth beer.
Racing ends.
Chad says how'd it go out there?
Chad says you may be too small.
Chad looks straight ahead.
Six twenty, fifth beer.
It's June now.
Longest day of the year.
Back outside.
Ball up.
Ball down.
Back inside.
Six fifty, sixth beer.
Mama's coming home.
Maureen's coming home.
I thought mama can do better than Chad.
I thought this can't be all.
I thought about dad.
Mama shows up.
Maureen shows up.
TV keeps going.
Chad keeps watching.
Chad says hey babe to whoever listens.
Chad says how'd it go today to whoever listens.
It's almost supper.
Summer, so whatever.
It's all the same.

Melinda

Chad took me out Friday. He's still not supposed to drive, and I don't wanna open up that can of worms asking when he can again. It was starting to get dark, and we walked on down to Hal's for catfish. We went along for a block or so, slow and quiet, and all the air between us started to feel stretched too tight. Like a drum about ready to pop, and like someone needed to say something soon. A few fireflies danced and hovered around one of the yards to our left, and the woman that lived there ambled up her cracked driveway and slowly pulled the day's mail from the mailbox. It was only 7:45 and she was already in her housecoat. A pink and gray tattered thing, frayed at the cuffs, her old Adidas flip flops sticking out just beneath it. She gave a strained grin with a half-smoked but unlit cigarette hanging off her lip. She sifted through the ad pages and then looked closely at the weekly grocery store mailer. Then she turned and started slow back toward her house.

Y'all have a good evenin', she said sweetly, turning back toward us. The half cigarette bounced on her lips and looked like it would fall to the ground, but it never did.

Yup, Chad said back, never looking at her.

I saw that picture of Ben and Parker sitting out, he said.

So? I said.

Well, don't you think with this new start something like that just brings up bad memories?

It's Ben's dad. And it's not your room anyway. You don't make those rules, I said.

I guess so, but I'd guess it'd bring up bad memories. For you.

What do you know about those memories? It's a picture of Ben and his dad. He can have a picture out if he wants to.

Just trying to be honest, he said. Just trying to communicate.

We walked another half block, quiet.

I tell you about Wednesday night? he asked.

No.

J.R. and I got into it pretty bad.

What? Why? I asked.

J.R.'s just always got these guys hanging around. One comes over from Gideon and another down from Malden. Finally got too much and I called him out in front of 'em. He didn't like it.

Why'd you call him out?

They drink all the beer, eat a lot of my groceries and they never clean up. Always too loud and stay too long.

You couldn't have talked to JR on your own? Instead of in front of those guys?

Couldn't wait. I'd had it.

So you just took him outside and y'all fought?

Basically, yeah. Picked him up off the couch. Those boys didn't know what was happening, 'til it'd already happened.

Is that normal for y'all? Just . . . a fistfight without talking it out?

In my world it is.

Chad—

We talked for a minute, Chad interrupted. But J.R. pushed back and then we settled it. Old school. Or I did.

I stared ahead as we walked on.

Seems a little much. Seems like it could be done different, I said.

Nip it in the bud, he said.

What? I said, turning toward him.

That's how I do it, babe.

Right then we'd arrived at the front door of Hal's. It was pretty full and you could hear the bustle of the place as the front door opened. Don Chalmers held it open for us. He's a lawyer in town, and I recognized him from the billboard on 25 southbound. His wife gave a condescending smile to Chad, then me. She smelled like lemon fresh Pledge when she walked by.

The girl that seated us was Debbie Manning. She'd graduated two or three years after me. I didn't know her but most of the town knew that her daddy, Charles Manning, had fixed the election for the county tax assessor position. He was running for it and had allegedly won, but then just two weeks later his wife Carla pulled the rug out on him, went to the county paper's offices, and threw him under the bus. This went down apparently days after she'd found another woman's pajamas and two black, leather masks stashed away in his closet. Soon as Carla found all that, safe to say that Charles lost her support. Worse, the other woman was Carla's sister. I never knew or even saw the woman, but word was that she drove in from somewhere in Pemiscot County once a week, usually on Fridays to deliver farm reports. Debbie rarely showed much joy, and I guess it all lined up the more I thought about that turn of events.

Debbie ambled her way over to us and got two menus. She wiped them down with a damp dishrag. This way, she said, not looking at us. She was half there, just staring out the window, then across the room. She led us to a little two-top in the corner.

I couldn't think of much to say. It was so loud in there that it'd have been hard to hear anyway, so I pretended I was interested in the baseball game on TV. Chad's shirt was pressed. He looked like he was trying, at least to some extent. I told myself I was trying, too. He ordered a Bud Light as soon as we got to our table, then told Debbie he'd need another pretty quick.

I'm sorry Chad, but I can't stop thinking about you acting out like that, I said loud over the den of noise. I had to lean forward, hoping that he'd hear me.

What?

I don't think you should act out like that, Chad. Just hitting J.R. like that.

Well, that's how we do it. He looked off and then back and me and took a sharp swig of his beer.

What do you want me to do?

Don't you think there's another way?

Between me and J.R.? No. No way.

Really?

Nooo way, babe. Him and those boys are a mess. It's my turf, too. I mean, come on, right, Mel?

He'd never called me Mel. Then he laughed uncomfortable, with a want that I might finally get on board with what he was sayin'.

Debbie came over to take our drink orders.

I looked over at the family next to us, and then I looked at their kids working on a coloring sheet together. Then came a collective blast of laughter from the group of ladies laughing over at the long table. I watched as they all took sips of their wine. They were all done up and most of them looked the same. Like they were created in the same way, in the same place, and had long been making all the same decisions in life. Some doubled over laughing, and some had their arms around each other, and all I could think was that some nights it's hard to smile.

Maureen

Melinda and him came back from Hal's, and I waved 'em out to the patio where I was already sitting. They came out the sliding glass door, and I could already see pensive air between them, but I just worked around it. I'm not scared of that. Hosted a lot of parties at this point. Try for a laugh or two and keep moving, I say. Ben had been watching TV most of the night, and I was already in my housecoat and winding down some. I'd already opened a bottle of white and was ready to share. I went in and got a couple more glasses, and the more they sat there quiet, I guess the more I'd try fighting it. Trying to keep things light.

Was it packed down there?

They looked at each other, shrugged and made sturgeon faces.

Yeah, they both said.

These are for sharin', I said, pushing my cigarette case across the table toward them.

Thanks, Mo, Chad said, taking one out of the case.

Newports, I said.

I know, he said, lighting one up.

He offered the pack to Melinda but she shrugged him off.

Ben do all right tonight? Melinda asked.

He's great. I think he went for a run earlier, watching old X-Files episodes since, pretty much.

Y'all want anything to nibble on? I asked.

Hang on, I'll be right back, I said before they could answer.

I went on in and got out some Triscuits and colby jack. I had a little of that good Lindt dark chocolate and broke some of it up and put it all on a plate.

I went on back out the sliding glass door and Chad had poured himself a tall glass of wine. Melinda was gone. At first I wasn't sure if she'd gone on a walk or just snuck back in when I was in my kitchen reverie. Maybe she'd gone to the bathroom, or just turned in for the night. I looked down at the plate and set in on the table. I straightened out my housecoat and covered myself good. I sat down and looked across at Chad. He flicked at the base of his wine glass and looked off into the night sky. He seemed calm even though Melinda'd gone in. I looked off into the night sky, too. I thought about how I want folks comfortable when they're here.

Melinda

On Thursday night the TV droned Matlock. I'd been reading some and had fallen into an evening nap. I peeked out of my room and saw Ben's door was shut with no light peeking out from under it. In my haze I picked up the remote and cut off the TV when I saw Maureen sitting at the kitchen island in the dark, flipping through her phone. She looked up and the screen emitted white light across her face.

Hey, girl, she said putting the phone face down.
    Hey, Mo.
    You all right?
    I'm all right.
    What's on your mind, hon? She poured herself a half-glass of wine and cozied up in her house coat.
    What's not, Mo? I mean, are Ben and I still all right here? For a little while, I mean?
    My God, girl, of course. Place is as much y'all's as it is mine. She spun her pack of cigarettes around on the island.
    You want one?

I'm all right.

Girl, what do you think about getting outta here for a day or two? she asked.

Of course, Mo. I think about that all the time. I mean, you and I could—

No, hon. Not me and you. Just you.

Me?

Yeah. You're wrapped up tight, hon. I can feel it when I'm standing next to you. I can literally feel your tension like some white-hot light. I think you'd-

Me, solo?

Sure. I think a couple days on a little solo road trip might do you good. Just some time to drive. Maybe listen to some music.

Where, though?

Wherever, hon. You don't even have to know right now. You don't have to know 'til after you've turned the engine over.

With what?

Take the car. Take it a few days. It's more dependable than yours and it's only got eighty thousand on it or so. It's good. Could use a little trip itself.

Your car?

I just filled it up yesterday. Maybe I can use yours while you're gone to get me to and from work?

Well, yeah. I guess—

You guess nothin', girl. I can see a bunch of second guess in your eyes and I ain't gonna let you refuse me.

Really?

Of course. We're fine around here. You need a break from this little world, hon. She threw her arms open as if she was not just talking about the house, and Chad, and the monotony of the back-and-forth with Parker, trying to take care of Ben. Her arms extended in a way to where she was talking about Clarkton. Our county. Our relentless sludge of days and nights.

Parker's coming tomorrow, right? For Ben?

Yeah.

What time, around noon? Like usual?

Yeah.

And how long's Ben gonna be down there?

Three days. Through the weekend.

Well, then it's perfect timing, she said reaching for her wine glass.

It is?

Yeah, girl you can't afford not to get away for a little while. God, I wish I could.

You do?

Yeah, but you get to. Here. She slid the keys across the island toward me, then went and got a wine glass out of the cupboard. She poured half a glass and slid it over to me.

To your trip, she said, and raised her glass.

I raised mine and gave half a smile.

To my trip. Wherever the fuck I'm goin'.

We laughed for a second.

You remember I drive fast, Mo? I mean, sometimes.

Yeah, girl. I know how you do.

All right, then.

I'd never figured a short getaway. It took the rest of the night to get used to the idea of some solitude for a few days. Maybe listen to some music. Maybe get out and just walk along a river. Options I'd gotten so used to not having that I didn't even know I was missing them.

Maureen

Girl was still asleep when I left for work.

   She'd left the keys in the clutter of the island, so I cleared everything off and put them right in the center, next to an envelope.

   Eighty bucks in twenties stuffed inside.

   Four DQ coupons just for fun.

Melinda

It felt pretty early still.
   Ben leaned in the doorway.
   I'm goin', mama.
   I could hear Parker's car out front.
   I raised my head from under the comforter.
   I'll see you Monday, love.
   All right, mama.
   Hey, Ben?
   Yeah, mama.
   I love you.
   I love you too, mama.
   I heard his steps through the living room, toward the door.

The front door closed, then the screen door, then both car doors.
The sound of Parker's car faded down the street. The house and
the stillness and the morning doves outside.

I thought about what Ben and his dad might do this weekend, then

I thought about Maureen's car and what all the day might hold. I rolled over and pulled the covers with me. I thought of all the lines in the road between me and where I might go. I felt nervous in a way. Then I fell into a dream where there were hundreds of blackbirds over the fields out back. Flying strong, in the early moments of what would become some manic, sideways rain.

Ben

On the ride down I looked out over the fields.
Sometimes it's hard for me to imagine how he's fought.
What I do know is Dad's fought a lot.
I know he's still fighting.
He gets quiet sometimes.
Like now.
On this drive.
But not the bad kinda quiet.
It's the kind where I can tell he's careful now.
And the kind where I can tell he's thoughtful now.
The kind that tells me every step means something to him now.
Action.
Reaction.
One night back during the drinking.
Back when we were all together.
Dad got home somehow.
Dad drove home.
Mama and I were asleep.
I heard the low rumble on the other side of my bedroom wall.
In the garage.

I rolled back over for a minute.
But then I still heard the rumble.
I got up and walked on out there.
Dad had pulled on in.
Dad had shut the garage door.
Dad had the driver's side window part way down.
Dad was sleeping.
The car rumbled on.
I felt like it hadn't been that long
But who knew?
I screamed.
Mama came.
Mama screamed, too.
We opened the car door.
We shook dad.
We shook him some more.
Mama screamed again.
Dad mumbled.
Dad was still with us.
Dad was real sleepy and came to.
Dad heaved a breath.
A real gaseous breath.
Beer and liquor and fumes.
Dad leaned over.
Dad threw up into the floorboard.
Dad threw up on his shirt and pants.
But he was still with us.
Dad's fought a lot.
Still fighting.
I love my dad.

Melinda

The coffee was still warm so I poured the last of it in a Flash Market travel cup. I went on and packed a small bag of clothes for a couple nights and took the keys and the envelope Maureen left me on the kitchen table. Sometime in the night, or maybe this morning, she'd cleaned her car out. She'd topped off the tank, vacuumed it out and left a few CDs in the passenger seat. There was an old atlas jammed down between the driver's seat and armrest, and I thought it'd be more fun to stick with that instead of depending on a phone. I reached down for it and opened up to the Illinois page.

Mama used to take me and Maureen over to Cairo around the holidays. This was when I was eight, nine, maybe ten. There was an old place called Magnolia Manor over there. A mansion. They used to decorate it up at Christmas and have a big open house. I hadn't been there since those visits, and at some point in the middle of the night, after Mo had encouraged me to go on this trip, I decided I wanted to see it again. I remember the house was done up like some kind of Christmas wonderland inside. Elegant rooms, smiling white-haired ladies in red sweaters, walking around with trays of hot cider and cookies. I remember they were always so nice to us kids. I wanted to see the site of those memories with Mama; see if the years had reshaped what I'd let live on in my head.

There were obvious big roads that took less time, but the more I looked at the map, the more I leaned on taking the smaller roads over that way. The rest of the day would figure itself out.

Instead of going over to I-55, I went due north through Malden, up toward Dexter. I saw Clarkton in the rearview mirror and thought of Mo at work. Thought of the staff at Hal's getting ready for the day, the folks shopping at the Town and Country, and the town moving slow and mundane into another day. I thought of Ben beyond there — what all he and Parker might get into this weekend. Then I looked ahead over the soybean and watermelon fields. An old school bus with the whole top cut off ambled along the side of a field to my right. There were five or six teenage boys hanging off of it, all shirtless and laughing and cutting up. An old man drove it along the flank of the field, and the morning had already seen them fill it with watermelons. The air was warming up fast, and around Bunker Hill the car got too quiet for me. I held the steering wheel with my left hand, and with my right rummaged around that stack of Maureen's CDs in the front seat. She mostly kept them in the open, no cases. I grabbed a few and held them up near my line of sight toward the road. Some of her usual suspects. Alan Jackson, Ricky Skaggs, Conway Twitty. I put those back in a small stack and grabbed the others. There were a couple CDRs with her Sharpie'd handwriting on them. Lucinda Williams, Emmylou Harris, John Moreland. I put the Moreland one in. When I pulled in to Dexter, I took a right onto state highway 60 going eastbound toward Sikeston. There was a megachurch on my right, then a few warehouses and small businesses that broke open into miles of fields about as far as I could see. A song called Cherokee came on, and it felt like for whatever I'd amounted to inside this parcel of skin and bones, muscle and blood, water and oxygen, that all time had stopped.

I see you shining through the treetops
   But I don't feel you pulling strings anymore
   I still use your old alarm clock
   Every morning I get further off the course
   And don't I hear you speaking in the noises of this house
   Airplanes flying over shaking all my secrets out
   Now darling tell me something I don't already know
   I'm aware of where to find you
   It hurts too bad to go

I crossed I-55, then over the I-57 bridge, over the Mississippi. I looked down at all that water rushing by and was reminded of its power. I thought about all the lives it affected for miles north, and miles south. I tried to remember the last time I'd even left the state. I swerved a little looking down at the water, then got back into my lane. The big river seemed larger to me now than it did during those holiday trips, and the land on the Illinois side dropped off into a mix of fields and inlets and swamps and woods. A couple of rust-red barges lugged and huffed along below, and I wondered what it'd be like to work on one of those. I wondered how you'd have to reset your capacities for patience and space. How sleep would be. I took the exit off 57 and curved around through a town called Future City, through an old tunnel and into the north side of Cairo.

It was already mid-afternoon. I pulled off the main road into a rutted-out Jr. Food Mart parking lot. I parked in a space between a primer grey F-150 and a tan Dodge K-Car that was packed to the gills with clothes, children's toys, and papers stacked all over the dashboard. There was so much stuff in the car that the only place a person could fit was the driver's seat. Before I could get out of the car, a waif girl in an oversized, dirty Miami Heat jersey ran full speed out the front door with a handful of something I couldn't make out. Candy, maybe. She was short and barefoot and ragamuffin-like, and goddamn she was fast. A red-haired, lanky, teenaged clerk in a yellow apron gave chase, but he never had a chance. I swiveled around in the driver's seat to watch the scene, and by the time I fully turned around the little girl was out of sight. The boy reached the edge of the parking lot, realizing his post was left vacant. He turned back toward the store. Right then a little boy in a way-too-big Adidas tank top ran out with a fistful of Slim Jims, M&Ms and a Red Bull. The two kids had a plan, and the clerk had fallen for it. Goddamn! the clerk yelled to no one. Goddamn, Fuck! he yelled, again to no one. The clerk bent down and grabbed his knees, panting. He stood up right and looked upward. Goddddamnnnn! Again?! he screamed. He started back across the rumpled asphalt toward the store. Third fuckin' time, he muttered walking by the passenger side of Maureen's car, never seeing me. Her!, he said, and went back into the store. I kept the car running. I thought about going on in and getting some things I needed, but then I went on and backed out of the parking space.

Parker

I picked it up while he was up in Clarkton. Considering all the miles on it, Jim Gideon sold it to me for pretty reasonable. His daddy Walker farmed most of the land flanking the abandoned drive-in theater south of town, and was retiring soon. Walker had owned it since it was new and I took him at his word that it had at least a few thousand more miles in it. Good starter truck, he said. He said he'd changed the clutch and the tires, but otherwise hadn't had to do too much to it. Said he'd been strict about the maintenance and upkeep, which lined up with his reputation around town as a farmer. Oil changes, filters, hoses, and belts. It was a silver little thing and the bed was sure banged up from years of use. The back-right end was dented in some above the wheel well. It'd been clipped by a gooseneck trailer where the farmhand hauling it cut a turn too tight. Alignment and steering were still good. New battery two summers ago. I gave Jim the money. Twelve one-hundreds in a Farmers & Merchants bank envelope. He counted it out on the hood, folded it up and put it in his shirt pocket, then shook my hand. He said call him if I had any questions, and I said I would.

I hid it behind the shed out back and covered it with two blue tarps I'd had folded up in the garage. I secured the tarps with rocks at the base in case the wind whipped up while I was away from the house, possibly blowing my surprise. I stood back after I covered it and laughed some. It was obvious what it was. Like wrapping a tennis racket and putting it under the Christmas tree. But who cares. Hopefully Ben would like it. On the way home I'd topped off the tank, then stopped and vacuumed it out and cleaned it up pretty good. I test drove it around the bypass again this morning before I went and picked him up. Everything checked out, and I was sure excited to give him his first vehicle.

I got home, poured another cup of coffee, and got ready to head up to his mama's when Rachel called. She wanted to come over. I had trouble trying to tell her that I just wanted to spend some time with Ben this weekend. I stuttered and felt myself sweat, maybe on the brink of another fit. But I stopped short and we hung up. I knew what I wanted to say. I just could've done better in saying it. Every bit of it.

Rachel

We hung up and I went on to the Kroger.
   Maybe it's too fast.
   Not time to be around his son just yet.
   I parked far and the heat hung strong.
   Cereal first.
   Then some of those sparkling waters.
   Karen Higgins rolled up on me.
   Her boy in the cart, three years old maybe.
   (What's his name?)
   Rachel, hey!
   Karen.
   How are you, darlin', how's the bank?
   Bank?
   Where you were workin'?
   I never worked at the bank. It's Hillen's now.
   Hillen's of course! Karen said, ripping a pack of Now and
Laters from her nameless boy's hand.
   Dammit, no! she said.
   She looked me over.
   Anyway, how you been?

I'm fine.

You look fabulous but your eyes seem tired, hon.

I'm fine.

I see. Anyway, y'all sell clothes for teens and stuff, right?

At Hillen's, yeah.

Well would yall's store be a good store for, see, my niece Kerri Ann is in town and we got this dress up thing and well, she's not exactly a little girl any—

Starter bras?

You have 'em? Karen whispered, looking over her shoulder like it was taboo to talk about starter bras.

Yeah.

Oh gooooood. Great, I mean.

Yeah.

Great.

Yeah. Great. Starter bras are great.

Okay, hon. We'll go. Just wanted to ask before I took Kerri Ann down there. It's a big deal and my god she hates the thought of goin', but anyway . . .

Great. I looked at her little boy, who was now trying to get Karen's attention.

Hey, did I hear about you and Parker—

Maybe, I said, interrupting.

Ooh.

Ooh, what?

Just. Oh. I guess! That's nice, Rachel. I'll see you around.

She fussed with her coupons and tended to her little boy. He stretched and arched out from the child's seat toward the row of pickles.

I pushed my buggy away from them, on down the aisle.

Maybe I was moving too fast, I thought.

I wanna share with Parker, I thought. Build something.

But the way we been behavin'.

In cars.

On golf courses.

Farm roads.

Parking lots.

Lunch breaks.

All these strange, sticky afternoons. Blurring together.
Dead on.
We could make something good together.
But maybe he's ashamed.
Some days maybe I am, too.
Ice cream.
Coffee.
Nail polish remover.
Benadryl.
Sparkling waters.
I rounded toward the checkout.
Two registers open.
Four carts deep a piece.
Karen and her boy right in front of me.
Had to say hi and bye again, which I hated doing.

Melinda

I drove on south toward downtown Cairo. Highway 51 gave way to Washington Street, and the speed limit dropped to 25. Since getting off the interstate, all I'd seen was decline. We had that back in Clarkton and most of the other towns around us, but this was a different-looking thing. Older. Quiet and rutted out. Beautiful, historic buildings that I could tell were once cared for in some other, far time. Levees on each side and bridges going around the town now up to the north and down south. I wondered how it went wrong, and why. Maybe this town was supposed to unify the four states it basically intersected. Maybe they had hopes in lines of that. Now it was just some once-pulsating thread of industry and life left to die on its own peninsula. I remembered it all different back when Mama brought me. That's not to say it was all that different. It's just I remembered it as something other than this. Maybe Mama's joy and energy on those trips eclipsed all this fallout and wreckage. Maybe this town was already gone, even then. There's no hospital. Empty storefronts. Some lonely, larger sibling of Clarkton or Piggott or Hayti or Blytheville. West Memphis, too. And I'd heard all about East St. Louis. I realized all these towns had been in my family's direct line of sight for three generations. Left behind, heaving half a century's worth of stale and dying breath. Like a hurt wolf trying to catch up to the pack, falling further behind. All my life this was more or less the only kind of place I'd ever known.

I stopped in at Dollar General and asked the girl behind the counter about Magnolia Manor.

Aw God, girl it's sure a thing to see. Crown gem of Cairo. It's a grand mansion and you can go in an' see what it was like back then.

It's still nice?

Yeah. And like time travel. You just gotta hold on and go with it to the old times, just trust me, girl. My aunt works there giving tours some and minding the place. It's nice. Rest of this town's fallen apart, but Magnolia's nice.

My mama used to take me there when I was little, I said.

She did?! Mine, too.

The ladies in the—

Red sweaters?! Yes, they still do that but the crowds have fallen off. How long you here for?

I don't really know. Just passin' th—

You need yer hair done in town, well then I'd say Bee-Luv-Lee. My mama works there. Has since I was five.

I'm fine, I don't think I—

Anyway, girl, you beautiful.

Thanks, I said.

Like, in a hard-workin', don't-take-no-shit kinda way.

She laughed after she'd said it.

I am? Than—

Like, scary a little, but beautiful. Where you from?

Just across the riv—

I'm Carrie.

She took a long drink off a 32-ounce Jr. Food Mart mug and checked her phone.

I'm Melinda. I'm from across the river some.

Where again?

Clarkton. In Missouri.

Oh yeah, Missouri. Well I got a cousin in Sikeston.

What time does Magnolia Manor close?

Carrie looked up at the ceiling as if the answer would come down from the browned panels, then she looked back at me.

Four, I think.

I only had about twenty minutes. I decided I'd go tomorrow.

Any motels in town?

Yeah, there's the Cedar and there's the Quality Inn. My brother Tommy works at the Quality Inn part time. Does maintenance. It's on the up and up. I'd say stay there. No bedbugs, no whoring, stuff like that. Otherwise you're lookin' at Charleston or Ullin or even back over in Sikeston.

Thanks, Carrie. I appreciate it. Feels good to—

Look, me and Tommy and some friends from around are meetin' up at Spirit House later for beers if you wanna join. I mean, if you stay in town. Probably around 9.

Thanks, Carrie, I appreciate it. I'm still not sure what I'm—

Before I could make up an excuse she released about four inches of receipt paper from the register, wrote her number on it and slid it across the counter.

Ben

Early evening, dad had me go out back to get the mower.
  We'd been out in town most of the afternoon.
  He wanted me to cut the grass before it got too dark.
  There wasn't much time before sunset.
  I went on across the back yard toward the shed.
  I rounded the far corner of the shed.
  I saw a big blue tarp covering something.
  I stopped there for a sec.
  I turned back toward the house.
  I didn't see any movement.
  Then I turned back toward the tarp.
  Then back toward the house.
  Dad was trying to hide behind a tree.
  But he was real conspicuous.
  He was smiling.
  I knew.
  He knew I knew.
  Dad couldn't hold his excitement.
  I turned back toward the tarp, then back toward Dad.
  I heaved a single laugh from my gut.

Like I'd won a championship.
Like I'd won something at least.
Dad did, too.
He ran over.
We peeled the tarp back.
I looked over the truck.
I think he was as excited as I was.
Maybe more.
I think I'm responsible enough.
I think I can handle it.
I hugged my dad tight.
The mowing could wait.

Maureen

Always knew his knock. He was like a grackle to grass being cut, timing always right on. Hardly ever called Melinda or me in advance. He'd just show up. It was after supper. I'd had two glasses of wine already and even though I'd only been home from work a couple hours, the house already felt too quiet. I opened the front door and there he was.

She take off?

Yeah. I let her use my car for a little road trip. Just some time away to herself. Come on in.

I stepped out of the way and opened up the screen door with my left hand. He came on in.

She go down to see her old man?

I don't know, Chad.

Well, where'd she go? Called a few times already.

She didn't say where she was goin' and I don't think she had a set plan. Just a couple days and nights away. Time to herself.

Girl don't tell me nothin'.

She need to?

Hell yeah she needs—

Hon, you may or may not know that Melinda ain't had any time alone in ages. You may or may not know the bigger picture

here and what and where she came from before she met you.
Before she came here.

What? Chad barked, incredulous.

You need to zoom out, son. Anyway, I think she was overtaken
by the surprise of the idea of having personal time more than she
was with the notion of joy from it. That's how it gets when it's
been that long.

What do you mean? Chad said.

You get some freedom and then you almost don't know what to
do with yourself. That kinda thing.

He stood there, gruff, vacant, still handsome.

You got any more that wine left?

I do. Got the rest of this bottle here and another in the fridge.
Few beers, too. Come sit.

We went out to the porch and took our usual places. The sun
had set over the soybean fields to the west, but the sky still gave
off a low mix of orange and pink and blue that hung on. The
smell of Bill Hillman's smoker next door filled the air, and the
Clement boys played in the backyard on the other side of his
place. I could hear Bill over there lifting out the grates, maybe
adding more wood chips, checking his supper. The cicadas went
on and Chad sat there, still gruff.

She say anything about me?

Hon, no. But this ain't about you. None of it.

Chad sipped his wine and looked off.

Goddamn, he needed work.

I reached for my wine and we sat quiet while a few faint streams
of smoke trailed across the backyard. Night had fully fallen. The
backyard glowed a pale grey-green under the lone utility light at
the edge of the property. Beyond that gave way to the nighttime
blackness into miles of fields. You could walk far enough out
there this time of night and lose your way. I'd guess like being at
sea and losing the shore.

One of the Clement boys yelled out For fuck's sake that ain't
how you play the game, dumb shit, and right then the other
Clement boy bowed up and slugged the shit out of the first
Clement boy. Their mama called for 'em, and they all went in. It
was getting late.

Melinda

I stopped at the Quality Inn Carrie'd told me about. There were a few contractor trucks scattered around the parking lot, a beat-up Crown Vic, two POD storage containers, and a panel van. An old woman with a name tag that read Rooth ambled out from behind a curtain to the check-in desk. She couldn't have weighed more than ninety pounds. She had deep red, curly hair that looked like it was just done at the beauty shop. She wore a loose, blue Quality Inn vest and held an unlit Parliament. The curtain behind her led to a family room where a baby was crying. The air smelled like microwaved spaghetti, and a TV droned in there behind the baby's wails.

How many nights you need, hon?

Just tonight.

All right, hon. She moved slow. Her arthritic fingers moved over the keyboard and a printer moaned somewhere behind the wall to her left.

She hobbled off, came back with a piece of paper, put it on the counter and turned it toward me slow.

I'll need your address here, and make and model and license plate number down here, hon.

She highlighted each area on the sheet with a shaky hand.

I went on and put Maureen's address.

I can't remember the license plate number, you want me to go out—

'at's all right, hon. Make and model is fine, Rooth said. She tapped the filter end of the Parliament on the counter, oblivious to the baby's crying, which was louder now.

There's no smoking in the rooms, hon. No pets either. Need you to initial here.

You wanna pay cash or card, hon?

I'll use this card. I think.

I held my breath as she ran it, then exhaled when the little machine started to spit out the paper.

Sign here, hon. You're down at the end of the second floor. Tried to get you a quiet room in case we get a big crowd tonight. She handed me my key card in an envelope.

Y'all usually get big crowds?

On weekends, sometimes.

Really?

Good god, fuck yeah. And most everyone's from here in town. Rooth said flatly. She flipped her hands up as if there was nothin' she could do about it, then put the unlit Parliament in her mouth and ambled off back into the family room to tend to the baby.

I stepped out of the lobby, grabbed my bag from Maureen's car, and went on up to my room. I was sweaty. I smelled the sharp cut of B.O. from my left armpit as I made my way up the stairs.

Big Friday.

Melinda

The metallic smell of warm A/C condensation wafted around the place, and my room had a dampness to it. Dark in there, almost no matter the time of day it seemed. The motel wasn't all that old, but it'd sure been worn in. I checked the closet and put my bag on the table. There were cigarette burns on the bathroom sink, and through the room I could smell the ghosts of drifters, cheaters, lone wolves and families en route to about anywhere but here. I turned the TV on to keep me company, then checked under the bed. I pulled the curtains and laid down, the late afternoon sun trying to seep its way in, like it was trying to let me know I wasn't alone. I thought about Carrie from the Dollar General. I wondered what her family was like, and what all kept them here in Cairo. As I drifted off I could hear the contract workers talking out on the sidewalk a few rooms down. Probably starting their weekend a little early, nicking beers from the red Igloo cooler I saw by their door.

I woke up an hour or so later. I'd thought I wanted to hole up here all night, but I was already fidgety. I got the keys and went on out to Mo's car. I drove across Washington Street, over to Levee Road and pulled over near where I found a cut through the trees. From there I could see straight across the water to Missouri. I cut the engine off, climbed on top of the car, and sat and watched the barges surging their ways north and south. After about twenty minutes, the sun set across the other side. I thought about my son and husband over there, and thought how over there was most all I'd ever known in this world.

I drove on back to the motel. There was a comfort in the smell of the workers cooking their suppers on two small grills in the courtyard. I felt a happiness in the low buzz of their communion. I went up to the room and paced around for a few minutes, which was when I decided to call Carrie from the Dollar General after all.

Maureen

We were half in to bottle number two and he was finally smiling some.

Chad, what're you doin' here?

Here? Just unwindin' and—

Clarkton. What're you doin' around here in Clarkton?

Aww, he said. He looked over his shoulder quick and then back at me, like some answer was gonna appear over from the other yard.

Home base. Old friends, family close by. Figuring my next step.

Next step?

Somethin' new. I figure by fall. Saved back a little money. Maybe go up to Perryville. My ex-brother in law works at Hibbett Sports up there. Said he might be able to get me somethin'. With insurance, I hope. Workin' for FedEx or UPS could be somethin'. Place of my own.

Yeah, but what do you want?

What do you mean?

What is it you want in the big picture? You been livin' with J.R., hanging around here. Chasing Melinda. But also not chasing Melinda.

You're her sister. What do you think Melinda wants?

Get outta here for a while is what I think. Like most any of us.

Well, then?

I feel like you're able.

Able?

I feel like there's honorable actions in your past.

Whatever. Chad laughed.

When he laughed, the plain-as-day insecurity of a self-loathing schoolboy cut through. I got a good look at it. A front row seat, and to my eyes it was a perfect merger of something foul and sad.

So what is it?

He looked off again, then turned back and spun the cigarette case around in circles. The smile dropped from his face and his eyes sagged at the sides.

. . . Get outta here for a while, too, I guess.

Melinda

I walked in to the Spirit House, and there were only six or seven people hanging around. It was all one room with a bar on one side, a small liquor store on the other, and a kitchen in back. Paneled walls and neon beer signs in the front windows. Three beer-promotion NASCAR hoods hung from the ceiling, and there were a few low tables and '70s-style swivel chairs in the middle of the room. There were a couple of unattended video poker machines along the front wall, and a dry-erase board offering the specials of the week. Several flatscreen TVs were muted with golf and baseball on, and Take Me Home Tonight by Eddie Money and Ronnie Spector played loud in the place. A big Mexican man in a green wind suit and white puffy shoes sat in the corner by himself, belting out every word. He had a black cowboy hat that he took off for the Ronnie break down, singing Be my little baybeeeee! His eyes were red and puffy, probably thanks to an early start on the night.

I stood just inside the doorway, and saw Carrie already seated at the end of the bar. She smiled and waved me on over in a way that was like we'd known each other a while. I wasn't sure why I felt so happy to see her, but I was. There was a guy sitting with her.

Girl, you made it!

Hey, I said, timid and still looking around the place.

What you want, girl? She was already rifling through her purse for cash.

Aw, Carrie you don't have to—

No, girl. You're the guest here, lemme get first round.

Bud is fine.

She called out to the young bartender and ordered two Budweisers and put a ten down on the bar.

This is my brother, Tommy Schanda, she said, motioning toward the guy with her.

He was wiry and handsome, striated from what looked like years of physical work. He wore a dirty red International Harvester cap and a faded black Pennzoil T-shirt that'd been cut off at the sleeves. His dark brown hair flipped out from under his cap, and he had piercing blue eyes that felt like they could cut right through you. I shook his hand and before we said much of anything, I looked down. There was a dog with him.

This is Rick, Tommy said.

He's old as fuck. Seen it all.

I knelt down and pet the dog, then stood back up.

He's half Shepard and half Schnauzer, he said. Then he laughed out loud.

I paused.

Really?

Yeah, girl, true fact. Ever seen this kinda mix?

No.

Who fucked who? I said, surprised at how comfortable I was in this new company.

I don't know, but you know the shit didn't happen without a chair or at least a step stool, he said. Then he laughed real loud again.

Tommy went on.

I found him on Levee Road by the high school about eleven years ago. Far's I could tell he'd been hit by a car and left for dead. He was rail thin and God knows how long he'd been there sufferin', so I grabbed him. Saved him. Made him mine.

I looked back down at Rick. There was contentment in his little face. His muzzle was grayed, there was a nick in his left ear, and he moved slow. There was a wide, blue canvas belt over the lower half of his mid-section. I thought at first that it might be something to stabilize his back, but then Tommy kneeled down and flipped a foot-long metal stem down. It was a homemade contraption. It had a small, flat base on it and reached to the ground. Then Tommy rises up and explained that Rick's left rear leg had never fully functioned.

I never had the heart to amputate and make him a three-legged dog, so he's gotta wear this thing when we're not out walkin' around or playin'.

That thing?

Yeah, he said.

Tommy, is it true what I'm seein'? You made a kickstand for Rick?

Yeah, Tommy said. My dog's got a fuckin' kickstand. He gets tired.

I knelt down and pet Rick again. I realized I was a state away, with strangers, petting a dog with a kickstand. I stood back up, trying to find the words.

He's old as fuck, Tommy said.

The beers arrived and went down easy, and Carrie ordered us two more. The crowd was rolling in and the place was a lot louder now. Tommy looked away to the TV for a second, then turned back toward me.

Carrie tells me you're here from across the river.

Yeah. Clarkton. Over in Missouri.

How long you here for?

I'm not sure yet. Probably just a night or so, I said, yelling above the noise.

You seein' family around here?

No, just drivin' around.

Cool. Well, we're all goin' up to Sikeston tomorrow for BollFest if you wanna go.

BollFest?

Street fair kinda scene. Happens every summer and we go up. Cheap beer, food, live music. Weather seems like it'll be all right. Our cousin Ronnie's band plays around four or so.

Really?

Yeah, Trek Warrior.

Trek what?

Trek Warrior, Tommy said louder, taking a long pull off his beer. They're called Trek Warrior.

I paused.

They got a CD, he said.

They got one? I asked.

They made one, I mean. A new one.

He turned to Carrie, who was talking to the young bartender boy.

Hey, Carrie what's Ronnie and them's new CD called?

Ronnie's band?

Yeah!

It's called who gives a shit ain't nobody gonna be that fuckin' into it any—

Shit, girl, c'mon! Tommy yelled, laughing.

Carrie was laughing so hard she couldn't finish her joke about Ronnie.

C'mon, Ronnie and them are good! Tommy said.

Carrie shook off her laugh.

I think he's wastin' his time, she said.

She turned back to the young bartender, continuing their conversation.

Tommy turned back toward me and looked over his shoulder.

Well, I think they jam, he said low, looking me dead in the eye.

What kind of music? I asked.

Ronnie and them? Mostly rock, originals and some covers, too.

Covers?

You know, other people's songs. Eagles, Petty. Some modern stuff, too. Foo Fighters, Florence Plus The Machine.

Carrie cut in.

Shit, Tommy, you mean Florence *and* The Machine.

No I don't. It's Plus.

I'm pretty sure they're called Florence *and* The Machine, Tommy.

No, Carrie when you put the CD in or the song's playing on the radio, the readout on the console shows a plus sign. It's definitely Florence Plus The Machine. Even the CD cover's like that.

Goddammit, Tommy sometimes you're such an asshole. Carrie said.

She dug through her purse, got out a wadded-up bill and ordered two more Buds.

Tommy looked off at the TV over the bar, then back at me.

It's *plus*, he whispered, intent on having the last word.

I wish people would pay more mind to details like that in life, he said.

He took a long drink off his beer.

Anyway, we could probably take the hotel shuttle van. Hardly ever gets used.

I looked at the TV, then back at Tommy.

You wanna go? he asked.

Maureen

We finished off the wine, and he didn't leave when he said he was gonna leave. Instead he went to the fridge and got out two Bud Lights.

All right, Chad.

All right, what?

Gonna stop grilling you about all this big picture stuff and you're gonna cheer up.

I am?

You are.

He smelled good. I was feelin' no pain, and at this point I don't think he was either.

You ever shoot a 12-gauge, Mo?

Good god. Once.

Why just once?

When Melinda and I were maybe twelve, our Uncle Burl took us out shootin' up near Malden one Sunday. He had a 12-gauge and set up some targets in front of this little dirt bank. He was safe about it all. Melinda and I shared a BB gun and we were shooting at the targets. Then Uncle Burl asked us if one of us wanted to shoot the big gun. It was so loud. I didn't want any part of it, but Melinda really wanted to shoot that thing. She raised it up and before she knew it it'd knocked her right on her ass. Black eye and all, and she cried for what felt like an hour. Uncle Burl took us on home and tried to explain it all away to mama.

Shot a .22?

Yeah.

Feels good, right?

A .22 does, yeah. Shot one right out into that field over there a buncha times. A few weeks ago at a big rat snake that came in from out there. He was at the edge of the yard, maybe four foot.

Whose .22?

Mine!

Yours?

Mine.

You sittin' around here with a .22 and not tellin' me? he asked, finally smiling.

Boy, there's a lotta stuff you don't know about me.

What else?

Well, I make a mean cheese souffle'. And I won District in the Girls' 1600, junior year. I like old Antonio Bribiesca records.

Who?

Right.

Right?

I think you think you got all of us figured around here, but you don't. You sit here with me but I don't think you know me. You kinda seem over it all, just lookin' for somethin' to do. Maybe Melinda represents that. Or maybe I do.

Shit, girl . . .

Anyway. I said I wouldn't get back to all that big picture stuff. We're all searchin' in our ways. You be you. But if I got one simple demand out of you, it's that you respect my sister and her boy.

Chad sat there quiet.

I'm goin' in for a sec. You need anything?

Yeah. But it probably ain't in there, he said, smug.

He jiggled his empty Bud Light bottle.

I'll have another one a' these.

I went on in to the fluorescent light of the kitchen and got us the last couple Bud Lights from the back of the fridge.

Melinda

Tommy offered me a cigarette, and Carrie'd taken up talking with some other folks. Tommy asked her if she'd look after Rick for a few minutes and handed her the leash. Tommy and I went outside and around the south side of the bar to smoke. We lit up under an old barn light that hung off the side of the building. Gnats and night bugs swirled around it and all the light in the sky had gone. We stretched and kicked the dirt a little, new again to the outside and the quiet. Tommy looked out across Washington Street and took a drag.

Why Cairo?

Magnolia Manor, mostly.

Magnolia Manor?

My sister lent me her car. I'm on a short trip seeing some places my mama used to take us. Earlier today I got it in my head that I wanted to see that place again. So I drove over.

Beautiful place. It's held on somehow. Amongst all of this.

He motioned out toward the street, down toward a line of abandoned storefronts.

I remember it that way. I mean, beautiful. I said.

Tommy turned back toward me. We were pretty buzzed. I'd barely finished responding and he leaned in toward me. He held his cigarette down to his left side and put his right arm up above me, my back pressed to the worn-down asbestos siding of the Spirit House. I could hear voices in the parking lot, but no one was in sight. He pushed my stringy hair out of my face, kissed me long and moved his right hand down from the wall to my jawline. He ran his fingers along my chin, and in all of it our collective breath combined in some twine of alcohol, smoke, and abstract, new need. I held my cigarette out with my left hand. My back was against the wall. I moved my right hand along his right forearm, then up to his shoulder. He was toned and I could feel the map of veins and muscle and a life of labor in there. I closed my eyes and surrendered to the widening warmth of his lips and face and neck, and for just a few moments these were the only things I could sense in our ragged, exhausted worlds falling together. I didn't see or feel anything further than that. Everything and anything else would be fine to wait.

Maureen

We'd run through all the beer. We were laughing about some story involving his friend and a car repo gone sideways up in Poplar Bluff, and he reached for the arm of my chair. By now we were drunk and laughing steady, and right after the story of the car thing he pulled me in my chair a full and fast couple feet left from where I was. My foot clanked the base of the table. I thought about how strong Chad was and I heard myself laugh uncomfortably. I thought about that sinewy body underneath that white T-shirt and thought about what it'd be like to hold myself next to his form, finally. Suddenly we were right next to each other. Chad slurred and stuttered some.

Come here, girl.

His eyes were reddened and he looked me over.

Damn, girl, he said.

He heaved breath of beer and wine and leaned over. He reached his hand up to my cheek and moved in toward me, and was sloppy in every bit of it. I felt my face flatline. In some flash all the life that had been blurry and sinful in my mind straightened out and came clear. I thought about Melinda again. In my head I saw picture frames, and a warp-speed timeline of the ride we'd had together through life so far. Then I thought about all the ride we had left to go. I thought about how I wanted to help her and Ben through these days, no matter how many of these days there were gonna be. No matter what it put us all through.

Then I reached up. I removed Chad's hand from my cheek and gently moved it down toward his knee. He sighed and sat back, all persistence gone. He sat there motionless and quiet. Both hands on his knees, looking out toward the blackish-blue dark of the fields. Some part of me wanted to give him a chance to speak, so I waited. A minute or two passed and he stayed quiet. I looked out toward the fields, too.

I'll say goodnight now, I said.

I moved my chair backward across the concrete and stood up. When I did, Chad turned slowly toward me without blinking his eyes. He looked straight through me. Some hollow, fallen gaze. I gave him half a smile. It was a smile that said I was sorry for him, and a smile that said he could go on and let himself out. Then I took my cigarettes from the center of the patio table and made my way on in.

Parker

We rode around in Ben's truck this evening, and it was cool to get to see Ben get a handle on it. He was careful, and we stuck to the back streets for now. It felt good to see him enjoying it. We got home and took it easy for a while. Ben read in his room and I half watched an Angels/A's game on TV. I dozed off and woke up to a call from Leon. When I picked up, most of what I could hear was a lot of background noise, and I could tell he was a little buzzed from his speech. He said he was down at The Lantern and wanted to talk.

I paused for a minute. I hadn't been there since I'd gotten sober, and Leon knew that. He'd long respected that, and that's how I knew this was something serious. I went out to the kitchen and grabbed a half-liter of Coca-Cola out of the fridge. I took a long swig off of it just to try and wake up some, and now I was nervous. Not about the possibility of falling off the wagon or being back around that scene, but about what might be going on with Leon. He'd sounded frazzled and hung up early. I got my shoes on thinking what a good friend he'd been. I went down the hall and knocked on Ben's door. I cracked the door, leaned in and told him I'd be back in a little while. I backed out of the driveway, sped through the neighborhood, and merged onto the bypass. I sulked some at the reality of going back to The Lantern since the bad old days.

I walked in the front door and saw Leon first thing. He was down at the end of the bar by himself. It looked like he'd been there a while, and before I even sat down I realized that I'd never seen him hang his head like that. His right hand was around his beer and his left arm just hung limp. It was like he was half asleep.

My God, I thought. I knew things had been rough with Lizzie's health. She'd been diagnosed with colon cancer a little more than a year ago. There were no greetings this time. Leon only looked at me flatly. His face was swollen. That told me he'd been crying a while. He said it was stage four as of today. He said they ran tests all through the afternoon, and it had spread into her liver and lungs. Said she was at Methodist in Memphis overnight and at least into tomorrow for more tests. More observation. Her sister was down there with her. Leon and Lizzie'd been together twenty-one years. Had four kids, ages nineteen on down to seven.

Leon and I had a lot of history over just a handful of years. While most of it had been good, I think the rougher moments are what have made us closer friends. When I was still bad, still drinking a lot, I tried to get myself home from The Lantern one night after last call. I'd started drinking at a cookout at Shane's that afternoon, then spent maybe four or five hours at The Lantern. I was way too far gone to be trying to drive home, but no one really put up much of a fight as I was leaving. I guess that told me I was good enough. I'd taken Melinda's car that night. I managed to get out of the lot, and even got the car aimed toward home. I got maybe a half mile down College Street, at least as far as I recall. Then I remember the white flash of a dog, or maybe a possum

jumping out from the right, square on with the bumper. I still
don't know what it was. Never got a good look at it, and even after
it hit, it still had enough speed and energy to get out of there fast.
I veered left to avoid it, crossed the opposite lane and put the car
straight into the ditch that split College Street and the sidewalk.
It was about four-foot deep I'd guess. I was tossed around in the
seat but awake the whole time. I managed to get my phone from
down in the floorboard to call Leon. He was still at the bar. Leon
says when I called all I slurred out was "fuckin' pawwssum" and
"godddddddamn" and "College Swweeet." He put it all together
and showed up within a few minutes with some others from the
bar. One had an F-150 and a front winch system. I had a cut on
my forehead, I guess from ramming it into the steering wheel,
and Leon got good pressure on it with a handkerchief from the
glove box. He pulled me out of the car and a couple of those
guys managed to get the car out of the ditch without so much
as another car driving by, much less a cop. I guess no one on that
stretch of College Street heard us. At least no porch lights flipped
on, and no one came out. If they did hear it, maybe they decided
they didn't care enough to come out. Sometimes people just don't
want to get involved, and most times that kind of thing breaks
my heart, but this time I found myself thankful for it. They took
Melinda's car over to Leon's, and Leon dropped me off at home.
Of course Melinda found out the next day. I had to own up to it,
and we had to get her car fixed. But thanks to Leon, things didn't
get worse that night. Thanks to Leon, I got to Melinda's and my
bed safe. Nothing looked good, but thanks to Leon and a few
others that night I got to live and walk one more day.

After Leon told me the news about Lizzie I swiveled my bar stool
around toward him. Our space at the bar was limited and I felt
cold and numb. Then I pushed the bar stool back and stood up
and pulled myself close to him. I hugged him strong. I heard
all the loudness in the bar, but no specific sounds. No detail. I
pressed myself to Leon's upper body and cradled his head. Then I
felt his new tears give way to gravity. They fell down my chest and
puddled in the pit of my left elbow.

Parker

I didn't see what set the guy off. I wasn't even aware of him 'til he moved in on Leon's space. He took his beer and poured it all over the bar. Then he smashed the bottle over the ice bin. It was all one move. That's when I caught up to the awfulness of it all, and that's when I really saw the rage in the guy. The sound of it cut through the room over the top of everything, and I felt a collective anger fall over everyone in the place. It was a thing where I could tell it had been long felt there was evil in the room. I was just late to see it, and the crowd had just tried to work around it. Ignore it, even, and hope the guy just went away. I couldn't recall a time ever when someone did something like that at The Lantern. Leon sat there staring forward. As far as he was concerned, it wasn't like it even happened. There was beer all over the bar. He just sat there, still in tears. I pushed myself back from the bar and walked after the guy. He was staggering toward the door but looking back toward me as I followed. He was cut. He looked strong. He had on a tight white t-shirt and what looked like cargo or military pants. Short hair and a strong jawline. He turned and walked backward toward the front door. He teetered a little, and at one point he put both his middle fingers up to anyone and everyone.

His eyes were unfocused and red around the edges. He'd had a lot. After he smashed the bottle, he started yelling at all of us. At least whoever would listen. Something about how we didn't know half the pain he knew and how we probably hadn't seen shit in life. Then he turned back forward toward the door. He slurred something about some girl leavin' town without him. Slurred something about how her sister was evil, too. I'd never seen him back in my Lantern days, and for sure hadn't seen him around Rutherford. I guess he'd shown up a powder keg. Now he was sure in the trench of a poorly chosen battle, all by himself. I couldn't find that anyone even got his name. He pinball-walked toward the door and steadied himself on a bar stool for a few seconds. He'd almost made it. That's when Tony P. raised up from the front window table and hit him in the back of the head with a tire thumper. It happened so fast. The guy went limp and went straight down. He fell down between the bar and the first section of tables. The jukebox played that Dwight Yoakam song Fast As You, but we all went dead quiet. Every one of us. I couldn't believe that Tony P. had even done it. After a few seconds one guy screamed Fuck yeah! Tony P.! Then another guy screamed What the fuck, Tony P.? Then a few others yelled and voices started to come back up some. I looked over the whole scene, then back at Leon. Leon started to get up from his stool to walk over to see. I looked back down at the guy on the floor. There was a stream of blood running down the back of his head and onto the neckline of his t-shirt. He groaned a little, but he wasn't moving much. His arms were pinned underneath him. Then I looked over at Tony P. He seemed to be taking in what all he'd done. I'd never once known Tony P. to take any shit. Never known him to carry a tire thumper, either.

It had gotten late. Leon and I leaned on the railing out front of The Lantern, and a few folks milled around and talked while paramedics got the guy ready to take to the hospital. One talked to Melinda's uncle, and the other two worked to help stabilize him. By the time they loaded him up, he was starting to come to. He groaned a lot. It was bad. I wondered if they'd have to take him to Cape or Memphis. Most folks started to file out and head to their cars. I got Leon to the car and drove him on home. He was pretty drunk by this point. He was rattled, but quiet. I could see that he was exhausted. I got him up his front porch steps, then got on home to Ben. He was asleep but his bedroom light was still on. I flipped it off and headed back down the hall toward my room. I'd call Leon first thing tomorrow. I got undressed, got in bed, and turned out the light on the bedside table. I laid there in darkness. My body fought off any surrender to sleep. I could still hear the whole scene unraveling. I could still see Leon's face as it happened. I wondered about the guy Tony P. had hit. I wondered what he was seeing now. I wondered if there was any good in him. I wondered what it was that had even brought him to all of us in the first place.

Melinda

The blue of the morning light brightened on the other side of the curtain. I'd slept sideways on the unmade bed, and couldn't unravel the details on how I'd even gotten back to the motel. I looked out the window and saw Mo's car. It was parked on the far end of the lot, slightly straddling two parking spaces, but it looked fine. My hair smelled like smoke, my T-shirt was lined with sweat, and the dampness of the A/C in the room seemed to emphasize every bit of it. Tiny hammers inside my head, hot breath of stale beer. I brushed my teeth, put on some cutoff shorts and a clean t-shirt and went down to the lobby. Rooth was leaning over some paperwork, and I searched for the coffee stand.

Over there.

She said it without looking, only raising a ballpoint pen in the right direction.

Thanks, I mumbled.

How's your room?

Fine, thanks. I stirred the sugar into my coffee and took a sip to check levels.

Commotion didn't wake you?

Commotion?

Them contractor boys, she said, still never looking up.

What happened?

Big fight. In 204.

A fight?

Two of them boys really got into it. Spilled out of the room and one was about to throw the other right over the railing. The boys in 206 came out and separated 'em. Coworkers, I guess.

I didn't hear a thing, I said.

State police showed and ever'thang. Wrote up a report and took 'em away. Lotta damage. In 204, there is.

I guess I slept right through it.

Lucky you, Rooth said.

I did meet a guy that works here last night. At least I think he works here. Tommy?

Oh yeah, Tommy. He's all right. Rooth finally looked up from her paperwork and was gazing out toward the parking lot.

He is?

Yeah. Does good work around here. Couple days a week. Helps us a lot. Sweet family, too.

Family?

Yeah. Wife Jenny and their two little boys.

Jenny?

Yeah, but I think her and the boys gone over Lone Oak this weekend. Tommy called up here yesterday. Said he needed the van today. Helpin' a friend move, or something'.

Rooth looked down and got back to her paperwork. Without saying anything else I refilled the styrofoam cup with more coffee, walked out to the picnic table, and lit up a cigarette.

It was early, but it was already hot and the river air all around me felt like some upward moving swamp. I perched myself on the table and looked across to the woods. I felt bad for not having called Maureen. I'd do that today. I'd get back on track.

I looked across to the corner of the parking lot and saw the maintenance van. It sat there by itself, no other cars around it. It had a sun blind covering the inside of the windshield, was rusted out at the bottom, and had seen better days. I thought about Tommy and Carrie's trip up to Sikeston later today. I finished my cigarette and went on up to pack my things. I figured Magnolia Manor should be open before too long.

Parker

I let him drive us everywhere around town that morning. I hadn't gotten much sleep, but didn't say a thing about Leon or Lizzie or the scene just hours before at The Lantern. Ben didn't need to know, and I didn't wanna derail his joy with tough news or bad energy. He was so proud, and I was happy he liked the truck. We went for breakfast at the Dogwood Café. When he was done, the server came to take his plate and he took a long sip of water.

Can I take you fishin'? he asked, out of the blue.
   I was thrown off.
   Of course, when?
   Today, after we're done here.
   Sure. I mean, of course. Where?
   Out at the floodways, cool?
   Great. You drive?
   I'd like to.
   All right, then, I said.
   He looked up at the TV, then back toward me.
   After all the times in my life you took me, I finally get to take you, he said.

Melinda

I got there a few minutes before Magnolia Manor was scheduled to open. The front gate was open, so I took a blanket out of the back seat of the car and into the yard. I spread it out under the tree and just sat and stared up at the place for a little bit. Mowers whined in the distance, and there was no traffic on the street. I was still hungover. I could still taste the smoke and beer loitering around in my head. The lawn was immaculate, and for all the abandonment I'd seen in town, it looked like the place had been cared for over all these years. The trim around the windows had all been repainted, and the grass was cut in diagonal lines. Not just some rush job of back and forth lines. This was all thought out and full of detail. Things started to come back to me when I saw the gazebo off to the right. I remember mama and Maureen and me sitting there after we'd had cookies and tea inside, still with most of an afternoon ahead of us. I remember it was the kind of winter day that was sunny and not so cold. Mama was in a navy blue pea coat that she'd gotten secondhand. She had a cardinal-red sweater on underneath and had worn a green skirt that day. She wore what Mo and me called her fancy hat on the drive over. It was a fake fur winter hat that she'd found secondhand as well. Mama was resourceful and stylish to the end. I remember she smiled down at us as we walked down the steps toward the gazebo. She was the most beautiful woman I'd known, and Mo had said that, too. I never went through a phase where I didn't think that. We hardly had a thing in life, and Mama was strong and graceful and resilient though all of it, far as I'd ever seen. The night before we left for Cairo we all laid out our Sunday best. She decided we'd go in style to the Magnolia Manor, and she glowed the whole drive over. I think not because of the adventure and history and sweet ladies and decorations and tea and cookies. I think maybe just because it was just us girls. Maybe just on account of a special trip together. Finally. Steppin' out.

A lady stepped out on the porch and waved. She was frail and well-dressed, and she moved slow. She called out to me that they were open. She didn't look like how Carrie had described her aunt. I think this was someone else. Still, I folded up my blanket and took it over to the car.

I went on up the steps, walked in, and didn't remember much at all. It was ornate and gorgeous, and there was an extensive library off to the right. I smiled half-smiles as the lady recited some of Magnolia Manor's history. She told me a few facts and dates that kind of came and went as I tried to get the memories of Mama, Maureen, and me right in my mind's eye, then the lady let me walk on through by myself. It was a nice place, but in all I wasn't in there for more than fifteen minutes. Not because it wasn't beautiful, and not because it wasn't impressive in its way. But I realized halfway up the stairs to all the bedrooms, all I was chasing was a memory of Mama and us. Not Magnolia Manor.

Ben

We got in the truck.
    The sun was beating down.
    I could tell Dad was nervous.
    Maybe not fit nervous.
    But nervous.
    His right foot twitched a little.
    He clutched his pant legs at one point.
    He looked over at me.
    Said your mirrors look okay?
    I said yeah.
    Said got your seatbelt on?
    I said yeah
    He looked forward and smiled.
    Like, everything's okay, son.
    Like, everything's cool.
    Like, let's go by the house and get the gear.
    See how it goes.
    I backed out and Dad kept looking forward.
    Like, I'm cool.
    Like, I'm not nervous.

Dad took a deep breath.
Dad had seen me do this.
Dad had been here.
I pulled out of the parking lot and onto the bypass.
Dad took another deep breath and looked out beyond the city limits.
Then looked back ahead on the road.
Said you're doin' great, Ben.
Then clutched his pant legs a little again.
I held straight.
Ten and two like they'd taught me.
Speed limit like they'd taught me.
Used my signal like they'd taught me.
Easy turn into the neighborhood.
Another turn signal like they'd taught me.
Dad took a deep breath.
Easy turn onto our street. Slow.
Watch for children.
Watch for dogs.
Another turn signal like they taught me.
Into the driveway.
Dad took a deep breath.
He looked over and smiled.
Like, everything's cool.

Melinda

I drove away from Magnolia Manor, went north on Washington, then cut over to the eastside Levee Road, turning north again. The morning was about gone, and the heat felt full bore now. On the left side of me was a set of train tracks running north/south, and on my right was the Ohio River. Wide and powerful itself, and just two more miles or so from making the acquaintance of the Mississippi. I took things slow. The road was rutted out and I didn't wanna take a chance on messing up Maureen's car. I didn't put any music on. I just wanted to drive in the quiet for a little bit. I thought about the past twenty-four hours. I'd gone chasing this memory of Mama. Instead I found another town left to die. I wondered if I'd ever see Carrie or Tommy again. I thought about how in a way I'd like to. But then part of me wanted to let that memory alone. Let it begin and end like that. Like I should have with that memory of Mama. Like I should have with so many things in life. Why mess with it, I thought. Just let a small stamp of time exist in its already-good way. Most times it can't improve on what it's already been.

I pulled the car over and found a clearing in the bushes that led down to the river. About fifty yards out there were three barges parked along the west bank of the river. They were all pointed in the direction of Memphis and New Orleans and the Gulf. Rust-colored monstrosities of steel and goods and tarps and netting, floating, all silent. I didn't see anyone on the decks. I sat down on a large rock and I wondered if the crew was asleep. Wondered if they traveled at night. It was quiet out there. About all I could hear was the lapping of the water on the side of the barges and a few birds in the distance. Beneath the rock I was sitting on was a scattering of smaller rocks amongst the weeds. I got up and threw a few into the water below me. I looked up at the feathers of cirrus clouds over me and watched two cardinals chase each other around in the short trees along the bank. I looked back at Maureen's car up on the road, and the hot weight of not really having any plan for the day started to sink in.

Ben

Dad had all the fishing stuff in one corner of the garage.
He got the poles and I got the two tackle boxes.
He always had several that he liked to bring.
I had an old Zebco 808 Boss Hawg.
Dad got it for me when I was ten.
I'd tried others.
Expensive ones.
But I just loved the Boss Hawg.
It had always done well for me.
It wasn't fussy.
It wasn't fancy.
But it was lucky.
I knew it.
I always took care of it.
And it mostly took care of me.

Melinda

I picked up a few rocks and looked out toward the barge closest to me. It was a good ways out, but the way I'd thrown the first few, I thought maybe I could hit it. I figured I'd take three shots. If I could hit it with all three rocks, I'd drive east over to Metropolis. There was a Harrah's casino over there that I'd heard about. It was by the river, and I heard they always had cheap, nice rooms. If I could hit it with two, I'd go south toward Memphis. And if I hit it with one, I'd head back toward Mark Twain National Park. I hadn't been that direction since I was a kid, and I remember liking it. If I didn't hit it with any of 'em, well then I'd reset entirely. Start from scratch and think of something else.

The wind blew through my hair and I pushed it out of my face. I rolled my T-shirt sleeves up and stretched out my right arm like I'd seen baseball pitchers do before games. The way they stretch the arm horizontal, in the opposite direction across the front of their chest. I looked out toward the barge. Then I looked back at the car. I was thankful again to Maureen for letting me have a couple days away. Life was new and mostly quiet out here in my own head. But the truth was I felt pretty good.

Parker

We stopped at the Quik-Mart and got Cokes and waters and pretzels and worms. Ben did great driving out there. I rode shotgun, and I felt happy that this was the beginning of a new chapter for him. He pulled off the main highway at the floodway ditches, and we took the one-lane dirt road running north, right alongside the center ditch. There were a few people out fishing but it was getting late into the day where most folks had cleared out. We had a few favorite spots out there through his childhood years, and I knew where he was going without having to ask. Catfish sure bit out here, even later in the days.

We grabbed everything out of the back of the truck and walked down toward the clearing on the bank. Right then my phone rang. Ben headed on down to the ditch. I told him I'd be right there and picked up. I didn't feel like it was gonna be good, so I turned in the direction opposite Ben. Before I could say hello she started in on me.

What is it?

What?

You heard me.

Rachel?

Goddamn, yes, Parker. It's Rachel, now what is it?

What do you mean? I asked.

Ashamed?

Of what?

Me!

I—

Were we not gonna see each other this weekend?

I've got my son all—

'the fuck are we even doin' here?

Well, Ben and I are out fishin' and we—

Something's holding you back.

Holding me back from wha—

Taking me around, from letting me meet your son.

Nothing's holding me—

C'mon, Parker. Don't you think it's time to— . . . are . . . are we not anything? Don't you think we have something?

Rachel, we're just out fishin' and I was gonna—

You were gonna what, she shot back, cutting me off.

There was a pretty long pause. The truth is I wasn't sure what I was gonna do. I only knew I wanted to fish with Ben. Right then I felt it rising up from my feet like some hideous, untameable atomic power. Some desperate way to inventory what this energy was, or had been, with her. A too-familiar bolt struck inside of me. I started to tell her I'd call her right back, and that old white heat took back over. I'd been on a good run, but that was all done now. I threw the phone in the grass beside me and looked up in the air and howled. I heaved a breath and looked back down across the ditch. I felt Ben look back toward me.

Aww, did that bug you?!
  Bug you, shrug you?!
  Girl gone old swan!
  What a bad song!
  Bad song sad song all gone!

Melinda

The wind was whirling around a little more now. I held the three rocks in my left hand and made some space on the bank to get a running start for the first throw. I took four steps and heaved the first one as hard as I could. My left foot slid in the mud leading down to the water, but I got my footing back fast enough to avoid sliding all the way in. I watched the rock fly. It made a clank off the side of the barge, right at the base where the steel met the water. I could see the mark it left in the paint. I heard it clank, so it counted. One down.

I went back up to my starting point. I'd try for better footing. I scooted over just a little to avoid landing in that same muddy spot. I took another four steps, and landed steadier this time in a small patch of grass. I watched the second rock fly. It clanked off the side of the barge, about two feet up from where the water met the boat. Maybe some wind got behind it, or maybe I was finally warmed up. Two down.

I noted the grassy patch where I'd landed and made sure to aim for it again. I thought that going over to that casino hotel would sure be nice, but for the better part, something kid-like took over. I wanted to prove something to myself. Something athletic. Something physical. I went back up to the starting point, and saw the indentions I'd left in the grass. I set my feet and took my four steps. I heaved the third rock with everything I had. This time I stepped too far on my last stride. My left foot overshot the grass and slid in the mud right as the rock left my hand. I went down further this time than the first, and felt the cool of the river water rushing over my foot and into my shoe. I looked down, then back up toward the flying rock. It clanked right at the spot where the water met the barge. Three down.

"Hey! Hey, girl!" rang out from somewhere up ahead of me. I heard the voice, but didn't see the source. For just a little sliver of time right after that last clank, all I cared about was that I was three for three. At first I didn't think I could do that. But I did.

Ben

The family fishing down the bank looked over.
    Dad was down in the grass.
    Knees to his chest rocking back and forth.
    Eyes darting around.
    Screaming all kinds of things for a minute there.
    The screaming stopped.
    They got up and started toward us.
    I waved them away.
    I said I think he's all right, don't worry.
    I said it's cool, don't worry.
    They paused.
    They kept looking.
    I didn't know if he was all right.
    I'd never seen one of these.
    Only heard about them.
    From Mom.
    When she told me about these.
    She was always calm.
    She didn't judge.
    Even in the most violent storm.

Melinda

A man came out from behind one of the gray containers up top. He had a navy blue jumpsuit on and was holding a large wrench. He said something back in the direction of the container, maybe to another barge worker I couldn't see. Or workers. Slowly another man in the same kind of jumpsuit emerged. They were both about the same build. Maybe ex-high school football players. They looked weathered, probably by a hard-labored, industrial life on the river. Their necks were thick and their reddened faces swollen outward. Dirty blonde crewcuts on each. One in the same. I wondered how long they'd been on that boat, and then I wondered how long they'd been watching me. They looked down at me on the bank like I'd fallen from the sky. The first guy spoke, waving his arms out, wrench still in hand.

The fuck you doin' out here, girl?
  I didn't say anything.
  Asked you a question, he said.
  You out here by yourself, girl?
  I still didn't say anything.
  He sized me up and muttered something to the second guy.

The second guy laughed and muttered something back.

The first guy rubbed his belly.

He said something else to the second guy.

I felt frozen.

I folded my arms, suddenly trying to cover myself. The breeze blew my hair into my eyes, I looked toward the north, then back at the barge.

They were still sizing me up.

Goddamn, girl.

Goddamn, what? I barked.

That ass, girl.

Fuck you talkin' about? Can't even see it from where you are.

I can just tell. He looked over at the second guy, laughing.

You can tell what?

Can feel it. On me, he said.

All you'll get is a thought of it, boy.

Fuck you say to me, girl?

I stayed quiet.

Jeans'd look good on my floor, he said laughing. He looked at his buddy for approval.

My guess is livin' on that piece of shit you ain't even earned your own floor, boy. I barked, motioning toward the barge, surprised at myself.

Aww, now! Ol' girl got a mouth on her, he said, motioning toward the second guy.

You got any more jokes, ol' girl?

I looked north up the river, then back up at them. I didn't say anything.

Surely you got some more jokes.

I looked down. My hair in my face, quiet.

Out here throwing rocks and damaging private property now, huh, girl?

Oughta call yer ass in.

You wouldn't do it, I said.

I wouldn't?

Naw. Not a little river bitch-ass like you.

The distance and the water made me feel safer, but I still couldn't believe I'd said it. All alone, out here.

The fuck you just say to me, girl?

I looked up and his broad face scowled down. His mouth tightened with anger.

The fuck was that, ol' girl? the second guy said, wanting to stick up for his friend now.

I couldn't believe I was still standing there. Who suffers this kind of shit, I wondered to myself.

I didn't say anything. I turned back toward the car and started to walk away.

Hey! Hey, girl I'm talkin' to you, the second guy said.

I turned back toward them for just a second.

I looked at them up there in the wind, leaning over that rail, marooned on that mass of steel. Lonely, tired, and angry. I wanted to remember their wide, exhausted faces. Two withering shells of boyish anger. As I walked up the hill through the weeds, I could hear them both barking from the rail of the barge. Their voices flowed together as one vulgar noise. Some nonsensical frequency. Caged dogs barking, all detail going, then gone. Then a howl, and a splash. I turned back and my ankles felt the pitch of the hill underneath me. As I stumbled, I saw the first guy in the water. He'd jumped, giving chase. He was belly deep, trudging toward the shore. Now a primal fear, pure and mortifying.

Hey, ol' girl I'm talkin' to you!

I felt an iciness form in my armpits and at the back of my neck watching him move toward me. Heat formed where my hair met my forehead and I turned back toward the car. He reached the shore, screaming toward me, breaking into a run on the sandy silt, muddy and drenched. He was stumbling around in the mud. I fought my way uphill through the grass.

I got my footing and sprinted to the car.

Come 'ere, ol' girl! he screamed. The second guy howled.

Ooooweee, the second guy screamed. Get her good! he yelled, leaning over the railing.

I got clear of the weeds and to the asphalt, wrangled the keys from my right pocket and jumped into Maureen's car. I fumbled with the ignition as he made his way up the hill, drenched in river water. The engine turned over quick. My hands shook as I put it in drive and sped from the spot. I could see him reach the road in the rearview mirror. A wet, screaming dog. His arms flailed and the hate in his eyes cut through me, even from that distance. He sprinted and gave chase for a moment, stopping in the middle of the road, doubling over. I kept the speed steady, checked the gas gauge, and headed north.

Maureen

I went by the bank and then the post office. I called Melinda but there was no answer. I went to Belk up in Malden to look at clothes for a while, and maybe get a new swimsuit. It was that part of summer where the romance of the heat was long gone. Too hot to feel energized about much of anything, and the dog days were pressing down. Even the neighborhood kids were staying in more now. I got home, empty-handed, and threw my keys on the table. The house was dark, and it was too quiet without Melinda and Ben. Chad, even. I wondered if he ever came around to understanding, once he cooled off and had some time to think on it. Even if he tried to give off like he didn't.

I'd had voices and activity going on around here for months now, and suddenly it was like the plug got pulled. I was out of wine and out of beer. I turned the TV on, cycled the whole way through the guide, then cut it off. The place felt solemn and sad, and I sat there in the A/C for a minute.

I had half a piece laid up from a long time ago. Cheese heroin. Back when I was experimenting. I'd do it on my own. Just a tiny bit here and there. No one else around, and maybe with a Saturday or Sunday on the other side of it, just to bounce back. I talked myself out of it. But then I talked myself back over. I went and got the capsule out from my stash in the fridge and set it on the coffee table. I went back to the kitchen, found the foil and ripped a small piece off the roll. I straightened it out and emptied a little from the cap out onto it, then grabbed the lighter by my cigarettes in the middle of the table. I held the foil up with my right hand and flicked the lighter with my left. I held my face right over the foil. I flicked again. Then again. I couldn't get a flame. I put the lighter and the foil down, then tied my hair back. I got up and found some kitchen matches in the drawer next to the sink, then sat back down at the coffee table. I struck the match on the side of the box, picked up the foil, and held the match underneath. I held my face back over the foil. The smoke started to rise after a couple seconds, and I made a small cone of the foil as the smoke rose. Just beyond that stitch came something familiar, comforting, and private. There was a warmth and an ease in my veins and muscles and bones that I hadn't felt in a long time. I shifted myself across the cushions of the couch, stretched my legs out straight, and exhaled into the dark and cool air. I let my eyes roll back, and then closed them. I tossed the throw pillows to the floor, stretched out and gave myself over for a few seconds, falling willingly into to some crevice of self-acceptance, and some long-awaited release. I took a deep breath, sat upright, then leaned forward again. I struck another match, held the foil up and inhaled the smoke again. I exhaled, and leaned back again. I looked out toward the living room. Beyond the blinds the sun cut some undying dagger of brightness. It shot through a heat that these days seemed never-ending. I heard the midday blackbirds outside, thirsty and scrounging, then leaned back again and breathed deep. A mower started up next door. Faint voices. A man and a boy, I guessed. New trails of reverb colored every sound. But that was all out there now. Out there in a world I'd deal with tomorrow, or maybe the next day. The A/C cut off and I looked to my right, over toward the hallway. Suddenly it was some threshold, some portal to black infinity. The rug lengthened to where I couldn't see the end. Like in some way that might finally lead out of this place and this town, and maybe these days.

Melinda

I saw Maureen had called and I'd try her later. I drove north, up Levee Road, then toward Metropolis. I had most of Maureen's cash left and I had my check card. I hoped I had enough for gas over there and back to Clarkton tomorrow, maybe supper and the room if the rates were affordable like I'd heard.

I thought about those boys on the barge. Wondered how long they'd been working that job, and how long it'd been since they had any time off that boat. Wondered if they had anyone to go home to once they got off. Or maybe life was just lived fully from the fronts of their brains. Like what I just saw. Just do and say the first thing you think of. I bet they lit their farts. And I bet they'd harmed animals. I'd known boys like that. I'd known grown men like that.

The Ohio spread out to my right and I drove up Highway 37 through Mound City, toward Olmsted and New Grand Chain. The road was rutted out in places and there was hardly any traffic.

I wondered what Ben and Parker were up to. I figured fishing or just hanging around the house, trying to keep out of the heat. Ben never said much about the weekends down there. Just that they were all right. Dad's all right. Dinner was all right. It was all all right. I'd gotten to the point where I didn't press him with it anymore. I wondered if Parker had fixed the place up at all. It was pretty sparse the last I'd seen. Bachelor living. The living room didn't have much. There was our old couch, my grandma's old wingback chair and a small coffee table. He had a 21-inch flat screen sitting in the corner on top of two plastic storage bins from Wal-Mart. I left all the curtains there, but a while back I noticed Parker had a bedsheet hung over the sliding glass door leading out back. There was a plastic ficus tree in the corner and since I'd left, he'd hung his old Dale Earnhardt mirror over the couch. I guess to fill some space, or maybe as a final fuck off to me. Have his way, finally. As much resentment that had lived between us, I wanted Parker's place to be a home for them. Ben didn't have much in the line of space at Maureen's. I was so mad at Parker sometimes. And he was furious with me, still. I don't think he'll ever forgive me. But I had to root for him. I wanted his place to be something good. I needed it to be.

Maureen

I got up from the couch and went out to the living room. I closed the blinds as tight as I could, then went back to the couch and laid down. I nestled my head into the crevice where the cushion met the corner and felt sweat break where my forehead and hairline met. It was as good as I'd felt in a long time. The A/C kicked back on, and I heard my phone buzz at the table. Maybe an email. Maybe a text from Melinda. I knew I should check it but I couldn't bring myself to get up. I studied the popcorn ceiling, and noticed the way the summer shadows played around the room. Again I heard the man and the boy outside. Then the mower. It was all some song to me. I closed my eyes and dug myself further into the couch. I felt my body relax. It felt like I was falling to the very center of the Earth. I dreamed about Melinda and me.

We were kids.
Jeans and white T-shirts.
Black Converse sneakers.
Summer break.
There was a wide field with deep, fresh rows cut into it.

We could smell the soil, dark and damp.

We couldn't see the edges.

In the middle of it was a jungle gym, old, flecked with different colors of paint. Layers worn down with years of use.

I climbed up and stood tall on it, and Melinda looked upward at me.

I balanced myself on the topmost part of it.

I screamed out To the Earth we all return.

I screamed out What were we anyway?

But some gone thing!

Some flawed movement!

Some slow cancer!

I screamed all that.

Then my feet gave way.

My weight pulled me through the bars downward.

My chin hit the top bar, and I fell backward.

Into the damp soil.

Then Melinda screamed.

Then I felt the cool of blood come from the new gash in my chin.

Then I felt the air hit the wound, finding its way in.

Then Melinda screamed again, kneeling over me.

Then I let my head rest in the soil.

Then I felt the stream of blood moving down to my neck.

Across my chest, wetting my shirt, and down over my upper ribs.

Then I saw the silhouette of Melinda's head in the afternoon light above us.

I could feel the afternoon heat of the soil on the back of my head.

Just some gone thing, I said real low.

Then I closed my eyes.

Parker

I was foggy. I noticed that family down the way looking over at us. I knew I'd had another, and sensed it was bad. Ben looked at me, concerned. He'd never been around one of these. There was no need to break the silence. I sat there in the grass with my knees to my chest, slightly rocking back and forth. The only sound was the water going by us in the floodway, and a few robins across the way in the trees. A truck hit its engine break out on the highway. The sun came down hard now, directly overhead. All the world felt brighter and, like always after one of these things, a lot slower to me.

Ben gathered up our things, and closed up the tackle boxes. We hadn't even dropped a line in the water. He got the poles and put them in the back of the truck. I sat upright, then stood up slow. After he'd loaded the gear, he came over and took me by the arm and shoulder. He walked me over to the passenger side, got me situated in the seat, buckled me in. I reached both my arms out and rested my hands on the dashboard. I could feel sweat all over me, and could see it coming through my shirt. Ben went around to the bed, grabbed a water out of the cooler, untwisted the cap and handed it to me through the window. Without saying a word, he walked around the front of the truck, got in, and turned the engine over.

He buckled in and turned toward me, breaking the silence.
    Let's go take a little rest, Dad.
    I wanted to try to explain it all to him.
    And I wanted to make him feel better.
    But I had no real idea on how to do that.
    So instead I looked straight ahead, out toward the floodway.
    We have any of those Cokes left? I asked softly.
    Yeah, Dad. We do.
    He left the truck running and went around back to the bed. The truck shook slightly as he rummaged around in the cooler. He came around to the passenger side, twisted the cap off and handed it to me through the window.

Ben

We drove south toward the highway.
    I thought about what Mama had seen.
    How she'd handled it.
    I'd call her tonight.
    I need to know what to do.
    We got on 84-West toward town.
    We kept quiet on the drive back.
    Dad was tired.
    He leaned up against the window and closed his eyes.
    I thought about the time when I was seven.
    I was at Quik-Mart.
    I went to the counter.
    I told the teenage kid working there I needed a pack of Levi
Garrett.
    The teenage kid said who for?
    I said my dad.
    The teenage kid paused.
    Then the teenage kid said that's good enough for me.
    I said how much?
    The teenage kid said three-fifty.

I gave him four ones.
I said keep the change.
I went out front and got back on my bike.
I rode around town for a while.
Hoping all the kids would see me.
Hoping none of the grown-ups would see me.
Pouch sticking out of my back pocket.
I was pretty cool, I thought.
I got it together, I thought.
Hey, Scott.
Hey, Jimmy.
Hey, Shawn.
Hey, Jana.
Check me out, I thought.
I went on home.
I thought I had it hid.
But dad saw it.
Peeking out of my back pocket.
Dad said what's that?
I said what's what?
Dad said in your pocket.
I felt cold in my body.
I got hot face.
I wasn't smooth.
I wasn't cool.
He said where'd you get that?
He said oh, really?
He said well, come with me.
He took me to where the yard met the back field.
Said lemme see that.
I showed it to him.
Said pull it all out of the pack.
I pulled it all out of the pack.
Said put it all in your mouth.
I put it all in my mouth.
Said how's it now?
I said mmmphhm.
Said you feel cool now?

I said nnnph.
Said you still wanna chew?
I said nnnnnpph.
I couldn't hold it anymore.
I bent over with my hands on my knees.
He said that stuff's terrible.
I spit it out and a stream of vomit shot downward.
He said that stuff'll give you cancer.
I vomited again.
He said that stuff will kill you.
I vomited a third time.
Mr. Rawls came out on his back porch.
Mr. Rawls looked over at us.
I vomited a fourth and final time.
Dad walked back toward the house.
He said don't do that stuff, while he walked away.
I stood back upright.
I felt the faint breeze cool the sweat on my face, then heard Mr. Rawls back door close.

He'd gone back in.

Melinda

I kept to Highway 37 northbound. The big river drifted away through the trees to my right, then out of sight toward the east. The land opened back up to corn and soybean fields, and eventually the lower end of a wildlife refuge. I drove with the windows down most of the way, and there was hardly a cloud in the sky. There was a long running swath of cypress trees running east to west where I turned onto 169. The shadows along the highway became longer and more prominent. I stopped for gas in a little town called Karnak. An electronic bell rang as I pulled the door open, and my eyes adjusted to the light as I found myself in a gray cinder block room. Only about half of the lights were on inside. The counter and register were to my left, and to my right were three angled aisles, sparsely stocked and full of the usual. Candy, snacks, motor oil, a few dusty Mossy Oak caps, some hunting and gun and People magazines, cans of Vienna sausages and Chunky soup, dog food, cat food, a small section of school supplies, and some toiletries. Beyond the register was a grill. It was dark back there — cleaned up like that part of the store was closed for the day. There were two booths by the front window, and a Bud poster with the Cardinals' schedule hung crooked on the wall by the door. The place smelled like a mixture of fried food and cleaning chemicals. There were no other customers, and the clerk looked caught-up and unstressed. He leaned with one hand on the counter and one hand on the register, looking out toward the highway. Maybe his mid-afternoon lull. He was older, lanky, with long gray hair. He wore a loose navy blue pocket T-shirt, and a red vest hung off his frame. He seemed to be taking stock of all that the day had given him, or what it might still. He had an ease about himself, seemed content in the moment, and there was something fatherly and wise about him. I wondered if he had kids, and if he did, what they were like. There was a small portable radio off to his right, near where all the binders and paperwork sat. It played Don Williams's It Must Be Love at low volume. I pulled Maureen's envelope out of my pocket and pulled one of the bills out.

Can I get twenty of unleaded, please? I pushed my hair out of my face.

Yes, ma'am he said, pulling out of his reverie.

Also how much longer it is to Metropolis?

Metropolis? He asked.

Yeah. This road goes over that way, right?

He turned and centered himself toward the counter, fully awake now.

Yes, hon. You know they got a giant Superman statue right in the center of Metropolis?

No.

Museum, too! he blurted.

You headed to the casino?

Just drivin', I mumbled.

What's that? he asked loud.

Yeah, I guess. I mean, the casino. Thinking about going there.

It's maybe another forty minutes, he said.

Where you comin' from, hon?

Clarkton.

Clarkt—?

In Missouri, I interrupted.

Oh, he said.

Well, Metropolis gets busy on the weekends 'cause of the casino. Lotta people come over the river from Kentucky. You get a reservation?

What?

A reservation for a room. You get one?

No.

No?

I never got a reservation for much of anything. I'm just goin'.

Well, you might call and make one. It's Saturday and that place is about the only option in town. Wouldn't want you to go all the way over—

If I can't stay there I'll find somewhere else, I said.

I looked out toward Maureen's car.

Or head back home.

We both paused.

I'll take a receipt, I said.

I can give you the receipt after you've pumped the gas, he said. See if the car takes it all, okay?

I said all right, and went out and put the gas in the car.

As the pump ran I thought about the reservation thing some.

I'd look at the map and see what else was around there. I sure wanted to stay in that fancy casino hotel like I'd heard about. I'd never done that before and I already had it all in my head. I heard the bathrooms were about the size of a living room. I heard there were robes and little bottles of soap and lotion. I pictured a big, clean bed and lots of channels to look at. Maybe even a view of the river. I already had every bit of that stuff in my head.

The car took all twenty dollars and I went back into the store. I got the receipt and walked the aisles for a minute. I looked at the candy bars and gum and wondered how much my check card had on it. I hadn't looked at the account in a while. Not since I was on Maureen's computer, maybe last weekend. There wasn't much then.

I rounded the first aisle near the counter looking at the jerky, and the man broke the silence.

So you're just out ridin' around, hon?

Yeah, I said.

All by yourself?

Yeah, I said, still looking over the chips and pork rinds and pretzels.

Long trip or a short one?

Short. A temporary flee.

Temporary what?

Just drivin' for a while, y'know?

I think I do. I used to take off to the upper peninsula of Michigan every few summers, he said.

I never been over this way, I said.

Really? Oh, it gets nice further east. Rolling hills and state parks.

I've only ever been to Arkansas, Memphis, and Tunica, Mississippi, I said.

Well, goodness, hon. You stay close to home.

I know.

Ain't nothin wrong with that. Lotta folks do. He stared back out across the road.

Family? he asked, turning back toward me.

Yeah. A son. And work. They keep me plenty busy.

Well, hon you're in beautiful country over this way. Little further and you'll hit Shawnee National Forest and Garden of the Gods Recreation Area. You camp?

I'm just in it for a nice place tonight, I said.

Where's your son?

Back home. With his dad.

I see. How's that?

Transitional.

I see, he said.

You ain't runnin' from someone, are ya'? he asked outright.

No.

Just . . . recent times, I guess.

What, hon?

I feel like I'm runnin' from the last couple years, I said.

We paused.

I don't know why I'm tellin' you this, I said, ready to take it all back and leave.

Well, that's all right now. I don't know anyone that ain't wanted to run from at least a chapter or two of their own story.

I stayed silent for a minute and looked out the front window.

I'm gonna head on, I said.

Wait a sec, hon. You got a proper map or anything? he asked.

I got an old one, yeah.

Well, here, hon. Take this one. He reached under the counter and laid out a brand new, folded map of Illinois.

I bet this one's more updated than what you got.

I paused.

Here. He pushed it across the counter toward me.

Thanks, I said.

I opened it up and found where I was.

How long you been out drivin', hon? he asked.

Just a couple days.

Well, this feels strange for me to say, and I sure hope you don't take it wrong, but you look thin. You eaten much lately?

Right then I realized I hadn't eaten since yesterday afternoon, before I got to Cairo.

Some, I said.

Listen, and again, I hope you don't take it wrong, but I've got all these chicken tenders and some catfish here in the warmer. I never have much of a rush on a Saturday, and you're welcome to—

No, I don't want—

It's not a handout, hon, he said, cutting me off. We just never sell through it all on Saturdays. Weekdays we do, but Saturdays we don't ever. Byron always makes too much in the mornings. We have to take it home or throw it out.

I looked up at him through my hair. There was a kindness in his grey eyes and in the crow's feet flanking them.

And I get tired of eatin' all this stuff anyway, he laughed.

I felt myself surrender half a smile. I looked out at the car, then back at him.

Y'all really just throw it out?

Yeah. And I'm tired of all this food bein' wasted.

I'm Layton, he said. He extended his right hand, and I shook it.

I'm Melinda.

He moved over to the warmer and grabbed the tongs.

You want for here or to go, hon, he asked.

I looked at the empty booths by the window.

I'm not in a hurry, I said. I'll sit for a few.

He pulled out a sheet of red-and-white checked paper and put it in the basket. He put two chicken strips and two catfish filets in, then he piled some fries on.

You want any gravy or ketchup?

Gravy, I said.

He pulled a small styrofoam cup off a stack and filled it with gravy. He wedged it in amongst the chicken and fish and fries. He handed it to me over the warmer and motioned toward the plasticware just behind me.

Y'all got toothpaste here? I asked.

Of course! Layton said.

It's right down that third aisle there among the toiletries.

Cool, I said. I forgot it. I'll get some before I go.

I grabbed a plastic fork and knife and two napkins and went and sat down. The booth overlooked a couple newspaper machines, five parking spots, and Maureen's car still sitting out there by pump #2. Beyond that was the highway and the fading line of cypress trees. Still no traffic to speak of.

You want me to move my car off the pump?

It's fine. Eat, hon.

I bit into the catfish and then the fries. All of it merged together in my mouth and felt like a gift from above. The warmth and salt and grease ran over the back of my tongue, and with it I felt a solitary and uninterrupted happiness. As I chewed I looked down at my knees shaking. My body felt a pure delight. I looked back up and ate more. Layton went back to the counter and went through some receipts. I heard Rosanne Cash's Seven Year Ache come on the radio behind him.

He hummed along and wrote things down. I looked out across the road, then turned my head back down and kept eating.

Parker

We rode along back toward town. Ben was quiet, and it was sure hard for me to figure what to say. So I just looked out the window over the fields and kept quiet. But the quiet only made the air in the truck more uncomfortable. It felt like I was back at square one. I hadn't had a fit in what felt like ages. I wanted to get out of the truck and just kick the shit out of the tires and the dirt. Kick the shit out of myself. Maybe I'd call Dr. C again. See about getting another appointment. I'd saved a little money since the last visit. Maybe McCarren would have some answer about my coverage by now. I could handle one of these fits on my own. At least I'd taught myself to believe I could. But I couldn't stand doing this in front of my son. I couldn't bear the thought of making him mad, and I couldn't stand the thought of making him feel embarrassed of me. We had a lot of days left in this life left together. I wanted to be a good dad. I hadn't been this upset with myself in a long time, and the elephant in the room had just gotten a lot bigger as far as I was concerned.

Melinda

Layton kept humming, looking over his receipts at the counter. I'd guessed his shift was ending soon and he was closing out. I kept eating. I looked back out over the banged-up parking lot. I thought about Parker and Ben, what they might be up to.

Parker would say the craziest stuff when a fit took hold. Like a lightning bolt hit him. A stream of strange rhymes would just fly into the air. Like some wild Dr. Seuss thing. I remember one time we were headed down to Blytheville to see a movie. I was driving. We'd gotten a sitter for Ben and were having one of our date nights. This was before the drinking got rough. A fit came on while we were on the drive. He couldn't get the map folded exactly right. It was one of those old, big maps with a lotta folds. Took up the whole dashboard, and thinking back I'm not even sure why he'd gotten it out. We knew our way to Blytheville. But Parker kept trying and trying to get it folded right, and then it just took hold. For a few seconds it was like he became someone else. Something else. Kicking the floorboard, arms flailing around. Like a wildcat in a phone booth. I pulled over on the shoulder of the highway and by the time I did, it was mostly over. It would always happen fast, and as much as he'd flail he never once went after anyone or got violent. It was all within himself. A battle. You just had to give him space and let it fade out. Some fits would happen so quick you'd barely know what'd gone on.

Afterward he'd always conk out. So much energy would get spent that he'd just fall asleep.

That evening, after the fit, he fell asleep against the passenger side window. The sun was setting off to the west, all the way across Arkansas and beyond, and I drove on in silence. I looked over at him as he slept. I wondered what these fits must feel like from the inside. I wondered if he ever remembered much from them. He said he didn't, and I could believe that. I looked back out at the highway in front of us. Without looking down I reached for his hand. I held it and felt the callouses from a life of work. He was warm, and I felt the exhaustion pulsating in him. I thought of our years and the things that we'd been through. Then I thought of how much I loved him no matter. We still had so much life in front of us. I held his hand all the way to Blytheville. He woke up about the time we pulled into the theater parking lot. It took him a minute to figure out where we were. He stared out the front windshield and reached for his wallet off the dashboard. His voice was raspy when he asked what we were gonna see. I said I wasn't sure what movie was starting when. Then I said it didn't matter. We sat there with the engine still running. I felt tears start to well up in my eyes and looked over at him, slowly coming back into the world, straightening himself up some, almost ready to go. I said the only thing that mattered was that we had some time together, that we were still pretty young.

Parker

Ben and I got home and still had some of the afternoon left in front of us. We weren't supposed to be home this early, but what was done was done. We left all the gear in the bed of the truck. We'd unload it later. We went on into the cool dark of the house, still not saying anything. Ben went to his room, and I went to mine. I turned on the fan, took off my boots and laid down on the bed in my clothes. I found the remote in the folds of the comforter and flipped on the TV. Golf was on. I liked the sound of it at low volume during hot days. I heard Ben's door close. A minute or two later I heard music coming from down the hall. He'd put on the Tom Petty Long After Dark CD I gave him a year or so ago. The sun beat down outside and the cicadas sang loud. I drifted off by the second chorus of You Got Lucky. The sound of it fit itself in just under the hum of the ceiling fan above me.

Melinda

A beat-up, maroon Nissan Sentra pulled into the parking lot. It was missing its front bumper and there was a donut tire on the rear right side. A big gal with long, stringy black hair and heavy blue eye makeup got out of it and stomped her cigarette out on the pavement. She looked like she was in her late twenties. She wore black sweatpants, a pair of worn-down Reebok basketball shoes, and a red vest that told me she was coming in to take over for Layton. She was on her phone, and I could see and hear that she was mad at whoever was on the other end. She slammed the car door shut with her ass and held the cell phone between her ear and shoulder. She had a forty-four-ounce Flying-J mug in one hand, and juggled her keys in the other. She was talking so loud I could hear it all through the window.

I said put the goddamn dog in! she yelled.

Just grab it by the collar and get the goddamn dog back in the house! she yelled, louder.

Well, did it bite him? she asked.

There was a pause.

Then no harm, she said.

Fuck him! she said.

No, no . . . FUCK HIIIIIMM! she said.

Especially if he gon' come over without callin' first, she said.

Just get the fuckin' dog back in, she said.

She leaned on the Nissan and took a long drink off her mug.

She paused again, looking off through the trees, then paced around slow.

Well, if he comes back over tell him he can come say all that shit to my face next time.

She slammed the mug down on the hood of the car.

Fuck yeah, I'm serious, she yelled.

Call me when you get the dog in and when you get the chores I put you on done. And don't be fuckin' around today! she said.

There was another pause.

I know it's Saturday! she said.

I don't give a shit! she said.

I don't care, gotta go, bye! she yelled.

She put the mug and keys on the roof of the Nissan, flipped the phone shut and put it in the front pocket of her sweatpants. She grabbed the mug off the Nissan and stomped her way in through the front door of the store. Layton said hi to her as she walked in, but she didn't say anything back. She went straight to the bathroom for three or four minutes. When she came out, she went to the fountain drink station, refilled her mug with fresh ice and Mountain Dew, and got back on her phone. I kept eating, pretending not to notice her.

Layton took his drawer into the little office off the main room of the store. He was back there for a few minutes. He came back out without his red vest on. He straightened a few things in the store, then came over stood next to the booth where I sat.

He looked over at the girl, then back at me.

Hon, we're all runnin' in our ways. But I think the main thing is to take care of ourselves while we run. Take care of each other, too.

Here, he said, handing me the toothpaste.

On the house, he whispered.

My mouth was full of the last of the french fries.

I tried to say thanks but only a muffled sound came out. I looked up through my greasy hair and gave him a smile.

Stay safe out there, he said.

Layton walked out of the store and crossed the parking lot, on past the pumps. He walked the near-side shoulder of the highway, heading eastbound toward the thicker swath of cypress trees. He walked like you might on a Sunday evening. Easy, and in no hurry. I finished my last couple of bites and watched him until he was out of sight. The girl that took over for him had calmed down. She switched the station and turned the radio up loud. It was hard rock. The singer kept singing about kryptonite and Superman. It was loud and shrill and awful to my ears all the same. The girl looked over at me as the song found its outro. Raising her voice match with the volume of the radio.

You like this jam? she yelled.

I shrugged. I only half-smiled with a mouth full of food, trying to give an unspoken answer that was true to myself, but that might somehow be acceptable to her, too.

Maureen

The white tiger couldn't see.
    Old hawk feather dropping down.
    . . . done in.
    . . . done in.
    Slow voice, old sound
    Gone song, from a blackbird
    . . . done in.
    . . . done in.
    Rest, come to me
    Please, rest, come to me
    . . . done in.
    . . . done in.

Melinda

I parked, walked across the vast Harrah's parking lot, and went in through the revolving door. A massive white marble floor spread through the lobby, and there was a newly vacuumed purple rug leading up to the check-in desk. I needed a restroom before I asked about a room for the night. A beautiful, short-haired black girl behind the check-in desk smiled and directed me to the restroom. I looked at her tag, took note of her name and said thank you so much, Vonda. I told her I'd be back to see about getting a room.

When I came back there was an older couple at the counter. I had my bag and waited a few feet behind them. Retirees, I guessed. They had a small schnauzer with them, and matching plaid suitcases. He wore a straw golfer's hat, a white straight-bottom, button-down short-sleeved shirt with cuffed navy shorts. He had on expensive-looking leather slip-on shoes that had tassels, and no socks. The woman wore a long, yellow summer dress, a large-brimmed white straw hat, and tended to the dog. She still had her sunglasses on.

What do you mean we have to pay for parking? he said.

It's the hotel policy if you choose to park in the garage, Vonda said.

Well, we need to park in the garage but they never said anything about having to pay for it. Plus we've got at least twenty-thousand tier credits. Diamond status, right, love?

Right, the woman said, still kneeling down toward the dog.

Do you remember who you made your reservation with? Vonda asked.

It was online somewhere but that's beside the point. Point is I don't wanna have to pay for parking. Diamond status, I don't think I should have to.

He became more stern and his voice started to raise.

It's only a five-dollar charge per night, but we do have free parking in the two lots out front, Vonda said. She kept her smile and continued.

There's a lot on the north si—

We're not gonna park it out there, the man interrupted.

Ok, then sir, you're free to valet park it or you can self-park in the garage for the five-doll—

How much is the valet? he interrupted.

It's ten dollars per—

We'll just valet it, he interrupted again. Not because we want to but I guess because we have to. Diamond status, my ass, he said under his breath, looking around the lobby.

All right then, sir, I'll need a credit card and form of I.D., Vonda said.

The man reached toward his rear right pocket, pulled out his wallet and tossed the ID and Visa card onto the counter. Vonda took them and started typing at the keyboard. The man turned and surveyed the lobby again, then looked at me waiting behind him.

His face drooped, jowls pulling downward. He rocked back and forth on the balls of his feet, then rattled the keys and change in his front pocket. His wife knelt down and talked baby talk to the little dog.

These people, he said.

Then he turned back toward the counter.

The counter opened up and I lugged my bag toward it with half a smile to Vonda. She smiled back, unfazed by the couple that had been in front of me.

How can I help you today, girl? You checkin' in?

I just drove in, I said. Wanted to see if you had any rooms available.

Oh, girl, I'm so sorry. We been booked for this weekend since April.

My heart sunk. I was tired and hot from the drive, and sleepy from all the fried food. For a couple days now I'd had a vision of taking a nap in one of those nice rooms upstairs.

She went on.

There's the annual quilting convention in Paducah this weekend and we get a lot of the spillover here in town every year. It's almost like our Super Bowl weekend here.

I gave another half-smile and looked around the lobby. I'd told myself I'd figure it out, but I didn't really have a backup plan. I drifted out for a minute, thinking of the drive home. I thought about just heading back. I turned and noticed two couples were waiting behind me in line, then turned back toward Vonda.

There's really nothing?

Hang on a sec, girl. Lemme check a couple things real quick.

Really?

Yeah, I'm gonna call over at The Lodge. It's our motel across the street. I wanna see if they've had any cancellations there this afternoon. Hang tight, she said.

She picked up the phone and called over.

I looked around the lobby again. There were a lot of older couples milling around, most of them were wearing pleated shirts and deck shoes and sundresses. The air smelled like a mix of delicious steaks cooking and perfumed oxygen. Most of the folks sipped out of small glasses through thin red straws, and servers walked around in black vests with full trays. I wondered what a quilting convention was all about. I'd never heard of something like that, but I guess there's a gathering for most every kinda thing. Everybody's gotta be king of some kind of mountain, I thought. I bet there were a lot of awards handed out. Quilting dreams made. Quilting dreams broken, I thought.

I heard Vonda hang up the phone and I turned back toward the counter. She leaned forward, resting both of her arms on her paperwork and offered a smile.

Girl, timing has it that there was a cancellation on a single room about ten minutes ago, so we got one open over there. Only thing is I suggest you move on it quick if you want it, she said.

How much is it?

Sixty-seven fifty-nine, including taxes, and I'll make sure they give you a late checkout if you like.

I'll take it, I said.

Sure?

Yes, please.

K, hang on real quick.

Thank you, Vonda.

She picked the phone back up and called back over to The Lodge.

Marlene? 129 still available?

Ok.

Uh huh.

Ok, she'll take it.

She pressed the phone between her shoulder and chin and typed on the keyboard, then whispered to me that she'd need an I.D. and credit card.

I reached in my front left pocket and pulled both cards out. I had them bound by a thick blue rubber band. I was nervous as she ran my check card. I wanted to save the rest of the cash, and felt mostly sure that I had enough on the card. At least I hoped.

She typed away for a minute, and the sound of the printing machine brought some relief. I guess I'd have a place for the night.

Vonda hung up with Marlene.

Ok, girl you're all set, she said.

She came around the counter and walked me toward the revolving doors.

All you need to do is head out these doors, then look across the parking lot just to the right. You'll see The Lodge just across that little divider road there. You can stay parked in our lot or drive on over, just whatever you wanna do. If you walk, definitely be careful of the divider road. People drive fast on that thing. Folks around here wanna get checked in and get right to the tables. Anyway, head on over there. Marlene's at the front desk. She'll get you all set up.

Thank you, Vonda, I said low.

It was hard to find caring people in this world sometimes, and I'd met two this afternoon I'd never forget.

It's no problem, girl, I'm glad it worked out.

Without thinking I put my bag down and hugged her. Right then I realized I hadn't hugged anyone in what felt like weeks.

Maureen

The very last of the day's blue light seeped through the blinds. I felt heavy as pewter. My eyes were open but I couldn't pull myself up. Buried in the crack of the couch. I hadn't even taken off my shoes. Hungry. After almost an hour of this, I sat myself up. Fully dark now. I flipped on the lamp next to the couch and took a deep breath in the low, gold light of the living room. I couldn't drive like this. Really woozy. I'd walk on down to Hal's. Maybe sit at the end of the bar or try to sneak a table in a corner. Get a burger, keep to myself, and try to regain my wits. Get something on my stomach.

I got to my feet and went back to my room. I put on a clean, white, oversized T-shirt and a clean pair of jeans. I brushed my teeth and tried to fix my hair a little. I looked in the bathroom mirror, but nothing positive cut through the eclipse of exhaustion. The lines around my eyes were prominent and my eyelids hung heavy. I had a thin crease across my left cheek from the seam of the throw pillow. I splashed some water on my face and went out to the kitchen. I flipped on the fluorescent overhead lights and rummaged through the refrigerator for a minute. There was half a cup of cold coffee on the counter, left over from this morning. I downed it in one gulp, stretched my legs, got my purse and keys, and headed out the front door. I felt so unsure of myself that I checked the lock three times just to make sure I had it right. I forgot my watch and my phone, and I never caught a glimpse of the clock before I left. Had to be nine or so by now.

I lit a cigarette for the walk, and the street felt warm through my thin-soled sneakers. Most all of Clarkton's streets, if they were even paved, were wrecked with warps and cracks. In the dark spots between street lights I watched my step as best I could. The world felt syrupy slow, and I wondered where Melinda was and why she'd never called back. I wondered how the car was holding up and if she'd already run through the cash I'd left her.

The green and red neon lights of Hal's entryway were rough on my eyes. It was packed and the noise from the crowd was almost too much. The hostess, Glennys, asked me how many, maybe just to be facetious. I was clearly alone. I said it's just me tonight. She chuffed and directed me to an open seat at the end of the bar.

Glennys was my age, had been married and divorced twice, and had three kids. Two here in Clarkton and another in high school up in Jackson. She was a big girl, and was All-State in basketball and volleyball back in our high school days. She had a bad limp from a four-wheeler accident while deer hunting up around Dexter during the winter of her senior year, and it ruined any chances of her getting an athletic scholarship, and a decent ticket out of here. So she'd stayed like a lot of us. The black vest of her work uniform was almost always dirty with grease or salad dressing, and though she was still relatively young, she didn't seem to have much patience or love for anything anymore. When she really got worked up, I mean really talking, little bits of spittle would gather at the corners of her mouth, and it was hard not to be distracted by that. In junior high Melinda told me that Glennys once rubbed straight turpentine on her dog's asshole just because she'd heard it'd make the dog cause a big scene and rub its ass all over the grass. Well, apparently it did freak out, and next thing I heard was animal protection services came and got the dog. Glennys never got it back. She'd never told me anything about her divorces or her kids or the four-wheeler accident or any of this other stuff. We were never good enough friends for that. Word just gets around. Word gets around in Clarkton without hardly ever havin' to ask anything.

She said someone else would be with me in a few, then asked what I wanted to drink.

Iced tea, I said.

She didn't respond and walked off, then came back with it about twelve minutes later.

Melinda

Marlene checked me in. I got to the room and threw my bag on the bed. It was a first-floor room and looked across the parking lot toward the big hotel across the way. I still thought about what those rooms over there might be like, how big and nice they probably were. I turned and looked around the room. Even though I didn't get a room at the big hotel, this place they put me in was sure a lot nicer than the one in Cairo. I sprawled out on the bed and stretched and pressed my head into one of the pillows. It was comfortable, the air conditioner wasn't noisy, the locks on the door worked and I didn't see any cigarette burns or smell any old ghosts of smoke. They had a nice robe hanging on the bathroom door, too. I got up and took my first shower since Maureen's. I shaved my legs, put on the robe, clipped my fingernails and toenails, and fell asleep on the bed to an old Maury Povich episode where some guy was upset that his wife had left him for his brother. All I could think was that I'd be upset, too. It was awful. I drifted off not finding a single way to blame the first guy. I felt the remote slide out of my hand and hit the floor, but I was too tired to get it right then.

When I woke up, I remembered I saw a street fair being set up downtown when I drove in. I put on a pair of clean jeans, a faded black T-shirt, and my old work boots. I locked up, crossed the parking lot and walked down the main road. It led right down to a large boat landing on the Ohio River. The red and white flashing lights on Harrah's lit up the whole parking lot and most of the boat landing. It was like a tourist beacon of concrete and glass and steel over here on the Illinois side. Just across the river were untouched, dark Kentucky woodlands. I could make out all the detail of the first line of trees just across the water, and it felt like I was paying witness to both the oldest and newest forms of civilization. Right there across from each other.

I headed back up the main street. Just beyond the Harrah's started a line of tents, and they had the whole street closed off. I could smell all kinds of food cooking. There were families and small groups milling around, strolling and eating, and there were two corner bars with folks spilling onto the sidewalk for cigarettes and the kind of loud conversation people have when they start to get pretty buzzed. I hadn't had supper yet, and as much as I dreamed of going into that big hotel and having a steak, I was still pretty full from the chicken and fish that Layton gave me. I walked up to an orange-and-green decorated tent where a big guy in Dickies coveralls was cooking and manning the register. He had wide eyes, a big beard, and a look of kindness that seemed built-in. I looked over the menu and it all seemed pretty out there to me. Alligator, fried oysters, elk burgers, kangaroo burgers, blackened this and blackened that.

You ever try some gar, girl? he asked.
No, I said.
Here ye go, give this a shot.
He handed me a toothpick with a small piece of brownish black meat on the end of it.
I just now fried it up, he said, smiling.
I took a small bite with my front teeth. The kind of bite that splits the line between curious and not fully up for it. I chewed

slowly and let the gaminess run its course. It was tough, and finished with a smoky char.

Is this usual, I asked. To cook up gar?

For me it is, he said. I get customers askin' for it.

Really?

Oh yeah. It's cheap and they like it. Carp, too, he said.

Here, try this, he said.

He handed me another toothpick, this time with a rounded piece of pinkish-brown fatty meat on it.

What's this one? I asked.

That's a piece of fried pig's tail.

You're fryin' pig's tails?

Sure! You never had it?

Never once, I said.

Aw, girl they good if you get 'em just right. I made these about a half hour ago.

I took the same kind of hesitant bite.

It was greasy and slimy and had some smoke flavor to it. I moved it around in my mouth slowly but I couldn't find a comfortable place for it. I couldn't tell the meat from the fat. I worked around the bone and it slid down my throat without much chewing at all. I pulled the bone out of my mouth and threw it in the trash can by the booth.

Thank you.

Sure, girl! Hope you liked it!

I'm Wyatt. He stuck out his hand.

Hey, I'm Melinda.

Thanks for stoppin'.

I liked his energy. At this point I wanted to support his business somehow. Problem was there wasn't a thing on the menu I wanted.

Can I just get a Coke?

Sure! he belted.

He reached into a cooler down to his right and got one out.

Coldest one I got.

Thanks, Wyatt. How much?

Dollar.

I paid him, and as I turned to walk he yelled out that the rattle-snake he was cooking was ready. The couple that had waited behind me closed in to check it out.

I walked on through the rest of the street fair and got a small burger and some sweet potato fries. I sat on a high curb in front of the Superman museum, away from the crowd, and ate it all. I watched the families go by, and could hear the drunks out front of the bar from all the way down at the opposite end of the street. When I finished up I tried to call Maureen again, but she didn't answer. I walked back toward the motel and called Ben. It was quiet enough down that way to where we could talk. His voice was music to my ears over the faint but powerful flow of the Ohio. I sat down in a small patch of grass and settled in, just beyond the motel, where the streetlight faded and the riverbank started.

Maureen

Every seat in the place was taken. Even once I was seated, I could see there were eight or ten people behind me waiting to get in. A few minutes after she'd brought me the tea, Glennys came back over to my seat at the bar.

Trisha's busy workin' those two sections so I'll get your order, what you wantin'? she asked, all in one run-on streak.

I'll take the chef's salad with chicken, and—

All right I'll go put it in, she said, and hurried off.

I shouldn't have come down here. I was still groggy, trying to keep to myself at the end of the bar. But it was Clarkton. I knew or had dealt with almost everyone in the room from working at the bank for so long. High school before that. And all the beaten-up years of childhood and adolescence before that. Ken Ray Stafford and his wife caught my eye from the other end of the bar. I half-smiled and waved. Then Jennie and Carl Mullins waved from their table. I half-smiled and waved, then looked away. Then Ronnie from the bank who'd tried to pick me up at the Christmas party last year. I pretended I didn't see him. Then Penny Joe Crawford and her two teen-aged kids. They were all tan and fresh and showered, wearing summer casual pastels. Like they stepped out of a fuckin' Belk billboard. Then Danny the bartender with the near-mullet who had the hots for Melinda the first time I brought her in. Of course he came over. He asked how she was and where she was, and I didn't have an answer to either. After he turned to serve someone I pretended to watch the Cardinals game on the TV above the bar. Right then I wished I had my phone or at least a book to look busy with.

Glennys came over with the salad. She put it down in front of me quick, refilled my tea, and maybe intentional or not, splashed a good bit on my left wrist and down off the bar. She didn't say anything and ran off to tend to a golf visor guy with his wife and two toddlers. One of the kids was screaming bloody murder like it'd been stabbed. The golf visor guy was grimacing and making the "check, please" motion with his hand in the air. Suddenly this whole town and all these people in it had bored me near to tears. I ate in silence, keeping my mouth full and my head down for the next fifteen minutes or so. After I'd finished my salad and tea, Glennys came by and uncaringly asked if I needed anything else. I said just a little more iced tea and the check, thanks. She came back with more tea and dropped the check off. She started to walk away, but then she turned back.

You still shackin' up yore sister? she asked in a condescending drawl.
    Melinda? I asked, thrown off.
    Yeah, you still puttin' her up?
    Yeah, why?
    Well, Danny, he told me a few weeks ago that she was still sluffin' around.
    Sluffin'?
    Yeah.

Okay, I said. Not knowing what she was getting at.

How long you gon' do awl that for?

Long as she needs, I said, looking over the check.

How's all that?

What do you mean?

Like, how's that work? she asked.

I swiveled around toward her on the bar stool.

Pretty good actually. We're closer now. Seems like—

Her boey, too? Or her boey go down yonder with his daddy? she interrupted, looking over at one of her tables.

He splits time between my place and his dad's.

That's gotta be tough on that boey, she said.

He's pretty well adjusted, I said.

Well, good luck with awl that girl, I don't think I'd e'er do that, she said.

Do what? I asked

Put up fam'ly adulteresses, much less thur kids.

You be you, then, Glennys.

She pushed on.

I just wonder if it woulda all worked out different, Glennys said.

If what would have? I asked.

If y'all still had anyone to help.

What do you mean?

Well, if yall's mama was still here. If yall's dad hadn't split.

Really? That concerns you?

Yeah.

You're gonna take this there?

Well, yeah, she said.

Mighta wound up different, she said, shaking her head.

What makes you think so, Glennys?

Just havin' some help. Some better raisin' around.

I can look after Melinda and Ben just fine.

C'mon, now. Whole reason they're even up here is 'cause your sister's pizzeria whorin'.

An unbearable heat came over me.

What, Glennys?

I wanted to hear her say it again.

Well, ever'one around's talkin' bout your place like it's some fallout shelter built on sin.

You're really being serious with me right now?

Nasty, sad sin, she said. She looked down at me . . .

She had her hands on her wide hips, and then tilted her head in that the-fuck-you-gonna-do-about-it? kind of way. The kind of thing I hadn't encountered since high school.

Glennys, you gotta live in your own skin. Hard for me to figure any punishment sadder than that, I said. Leave my fuckin' family out of your thoughts.

I raised the iced tea high between us, tilted the glass and let the whole of it pour down to Glennys's lower legs and feet. I felt cold splashes of it bounce off the floor onto my shoes. Her face was pure disgust, and her mouth fell open as the iced tea soaked her feet. I was surprised she stood for that long without budging. I set the glass down on the bar to my right, moved around her and started toward the door. I heard her say Oh shit, I know you didn't, and then something else that I couldn't make out. All that came out of her gathered inertia and volume, and then I heard her slam her tray down. Then I heard her scream Come back here, bitch. Then she said it again, louder. Then I heard more clatter behind me and I felt her on my path, but I didn't ever look back.

I felt a slow, hot tremor of everyone noticing, and saw myself out of the building. I still felt the ghost of the afternoon dope. Still tasted it in the back of my throat. I broke into a trot, then a jog, then a full-blown sprint back toward home through the dark streets of another fanged night.

Ben

Mama sounded peaceful.
   Said she'd seen some miles.
   Met some people.
   Had some quiet.
   I told her about Dad's fit.
   I told her how it went, mostly.
   She asked if I was embarrassed.
   I said I don't think so.
   She asked if Dad remembered.
   I said I don't think so.
   She asked if he'd had one since.
   I said I don't think so.
   Said she'd get back soon.
   Said she'd see me in a couple days.
   Said hang on a sec.
   Said I'm gonna hold my phone up.
   Asked if I could hear that big river out there.
   I stayed quiet.
   I put one finger in my other ear to keep sound out.
   I could hear that river.

I could picture the life around it.
Some world of its own.
In the dark now.
Far, but not too far.
It felt good to picture her out in that world.
Said one day soon we'd see it all together.

Melinda

My first thought was that the air conditioner had started rattling. I'd been in a deep sleep, but it didn't take long to realize that chunks of the wall were moving inward, toward me. I'd left the bathroom light on and the door cracked, and in the faint light could see the frame of the hotel room door bend inward as both panels of the window shattered. The lower segment of the wall and air conditioner got pushed further in and scooted the small table into my bed. The two little chairs slid along with it. The mass of furniture pushed the bed snug to the wall of the bathroom, and none of it happened very fast. I lurched upward and seen what was happening, and had reasonable time to consider that the back end of a running car was now in the room. Through the dust and exhaust, the red and white glow of the car's tail and reverse lights gave the mangled drywall and framing a dirty, peppermint halo. Then it all stopped. I crawled off the front of the bed, somehow unhurt. The car was still running. For a minute the room and the destruction was illuminated in brake-light red, until someone came to enough sense to cut the car off. The digital alarm clock on the bedside table read 2:17. I got my jeans and shoes on, and could hear a man and woman's voices through the lights just on the other side of all the dust. At first I thought it was drunk kids, but it didn't sound like drunk kids. The voices coming from the car sounded older.

I got over toward the door. The frame had bent in a way to where it broke the deadbolt and chain latch. The door was bent in a way where I was able to step out and over some of the rubble, out toward the sidewalk. A few other people started to emerge from their rooms. The car was a brown Buick Skylark, maybe early '80s, with no hubcaps and a primer-gray front right panel. A small-framed lady in a black-sequined, pullover dress made her way out of the passenger's side. She had a cigarette in her right hand, waving it around. She seemed to have the explanation all ready to go. She was tiny and slow. I'd guess at least 80.

Oh, honey. Honey, honnnney.
    I'm all right, I said.
    Honey, come here. Let me see you, she said.
    Her voice was low and gravelly. It reminded me of my grandma's when I'd call her on the phone early in the morning or late at night. I could hear it rattle around as she talked. She seemed to talk to everyone and no one at once as she got out of the car. She took small puffs of her cigarette and sips out of a well-used Kum and Go coffee tumbler when she wasn't speaking.
    I'm okay, I said.
    She extended her arms out and stepped toward me through the glass and drywall and cheap stucco on the sidewalk. I smelled whiskey and a full night of smoke brimming off her breath from a couple feet away.

Mamaaaaaaaah! Premium number one quilting queeeeeeen, 1985! a man's voice yelled from the driver's seat. I couldn't see him, only the silhouette of his shoulder and part of his head. She'd left the car door open. There was a wadded up Popeyes bag, a stack of wrinkled napkins, a few cigarette butts, an empty white wine bottle and a flattened-out mozzarella sticks box in the floor-board. I saw a children's car seat in the back. There was a little girl in there, looking out the rear side window. She was maybe three years old, wide awake. She drank out of a green sippy cup, and seemed unfazed by the whole thing. The woman waved her cigarette around and said it again.

Honnney. I am so sorry and you know we're gonna make this better.

I'm okay, I said again.

Martin got disoriented. I told him he had it in reverse and not drive, but goddamn it was too late. He just got mixed up.

The queeeeeen! he yelled.

Shut it, Martin! Get out of the fuckin' car! she said, spinning around toward him, then coughing. It was the fastest she'd moved yet. Her sequins glistened in the fluorescent parking lot lights.

Martin and I were just on a little date, she said. We used to be together, but we ain't no more. I mean, we still have our fun. He's married on. Third wife. Over in Mayfield. Anyway, that shit don't matter. I been lookin' after my grandbaby in Paducah all weekend. That's her. Opal. Wave hi, Opal!

She motioned toward the car seat, and the little girl and her big, brown eyes were still emotionless.

By then the night clerk had shown up. He was on his phone, I guess talking with the police.

It's baaaad, ain't it, Ray? Martin asked.

He slowly got himself out of the driver's seat, grabbing at his low back. He had a long, white combover, sunken cheekbones and wore a polyester brown suit with an orange dress shirt and navy blue snow boots. Matted, dirty fur stuck out of the tops of them. His eyes had a resting look of defeat. It looked like he hadn't missed a day of drinking in a long time.

I'm Raylene, the lady said. Call me Ray, though, she coughed long after that.

I'm Melinda.

There was a line of caked makeup that gave way to her dark brown hairline. When she bent over to cough, the breeze of her cheap-smelling perfume hit my nose. Martin stabilized himself, leaning on the back of the car. The night clerk confronted him, and Martin seemed generally cooperative. They spoke in low voices when Ray raised upright and moved toward me. The cigarette smoke and perfume was a constant now. She was in my face and talked in a low rasp, her eyes right on mine.

Now how we gonna make this better, hon? she asked, suddenly very serious. Dust and drywall still hung in the air.

I'm all right, I said.

She put her hand on my elbow and guided me a few feet away from the scene.

She started in.

Martin don't know this . . . , she looked over at him and paused, still occupied.

Hon, good chance Martin don't remember this at this point, but I won two-thousand dollars in prize money this mornin'. Best Large Scale Block and Patchwork and Best Applique, if you're wonderin'. He knows I won, but he'll never know how much I won 'cause all he ever did was mooch off me, and that's the main thing drove a stake in us. I'm self-made and better off on my own but we still have our fun as you can see. Anyway . . . she started, but coughed again, this time long and loud.

I can't . . . I started, but she interrupted.

Anyway, Melinda, we gon' fix this here and now and we gon' make this better. She whispered the last part, then took another drag off her cigarette. The little girl in the back seat called out, then started with a faint whimper that led to a steady cry.

My stuff's okay. I'm okay, I said. Just tired, and . . .

Ray clutched her purse, a small sequin thing that matched her dress, then unzipped it.

A thousand? she whispered.

No, no . . .

Fifteen hundred? She said it low, enunciating it clearly.

I'm al—

Fifteen hundred, hon? She whispered, then looked over her shoulder at Martin. His back was still to us, and he leaned on the other side of the car, steadying himself. The night clerk was still on the phone but asking Martin questions, probably reporting all the details to the cops. I heard sirens in the distance getting closer.

I didn't—

Here's fifteen hundred, hon. Are we all right?

I can't—

She pushed a folded wad of one-hundred-dollar bills into my left hand and closed my fingers over it.

We should be all right now, hon. Right?

I didn't say anything.

'else you need from me, hon? she asked. If so need you to hurry and tell me.

She looked over her shoulder. She'd said it through gritted teeth, and for this one sliver of a moment she actually seemed present. The sirens were getting closer, and she looked back at Martin. I realized I didn't wanna be here when the cops showed.

I only need three-hundred, I said.

I took three of the bills, shoved them into my jeans pocket, then pushed the rest back into her free hand.

The only other thing I need is for you to take the rest of this and take care of that baby girl I'm lookin' at right now. Opal?

Yeah, Ray said.

The little girl cried onward, her volume increasing with the coming sirens.

Okay, Ray whispered.

Cool, I said.

She wobbled back toward Martin and the car.

Two squad cars pulled into the parking lot. The cops got out and started their routine with Martin. The night clerk had become livid. His arms were waving around. He was bellowing and screaming. Martin just leaned on the car, not saying a word now. My bag was still in the room, but there wasn't a thing in it that was worth going back for. I had my wallet, Maureen's envelope and her car keys in my jeans from before I went to bed. By now there were a number of folks milling around on the sidewalk and in the parking lot wanting to see what had happened. Most of them were in their pajamas, and some were kneeled down trying their best to explain it to their children. I panned over them and only saw long faces. Once Martin, Ray and the night clerk were fully engaged with the cops, I stepped behind the black SUV just behind me. There were more cars parked behind it that served as a barrier. I stepped toward the sidewalk, ducking down and keeping low, moving away from the scene. A few cars down I raised up into a brisk walk, then turned into a breezeway, hiding behind the ice machine. It hummed and dumped a fresh load of ice from one part to another part of its innards, and night breeze off the river smelled of fish and rank mud. The breezeway beyond the ice machine led to a manicured grassy slope. Just beyond that the lights of the motel died and fell into darkness toward the Ohio River. I headed that way and found a dirt path leading between the motel grounds and the Harrah's across the way. I headed the way of the casino, and could see just enough of the path in front of me thanks to all the lights coming off the big hotel. There was the occasional bench and cutaway leading down to the river. A quarter mile or so beyond the Harrah's, I found a wooden bench and stretched out on it. I could still hear the faint sounds of voices coming from the motel parking lot. Distant cop radios. A child cried. Probably poor Opal, I thought. My feet hung off the edge of the bench a little but I didn't care. I took my shoes off, using them as a makeshift pillow and fell asleep fast. The breeze and the song of the old river lingered on eternal, right there in front of me.

I woke up to the sound of ducks over on the wooded Kentucky side. The air was humid, the back of my neck sticky, and the sun was starting to break through a thin line of eastern clouds. The sleep on that bench had been short, and my shirt was drenched from the humidity. I wondered what Ray and Martin and Opal were dealing with by now. I hoped little Opal finally got the rest she deserved. I pictured her sleeping, then I thought of Ben when he was that age. I'd put him down for the night, come back in and check on him a couple hours later and he'd be clear flipped over. Head at the foot of the bed, and feet on his pillow. Batman-caped pajamas all twisted, sweaty neck and forehead.

I felt my pocket for the three-hundred Ray gave me, and it was still there. I sat up, got my shoes on, and walked down to the water. There was hardly a sound, and it felt like from here, most of the world was still fast asleep. Early, but I figured it might be the best chance to catch Maureen. It only rang twice and she answered this time.

Hey girl, she said with a morning rasp in her voice.

Hey, Mo.

Where you, hon?

I tried calling a couple times already, Mo. Where you been?

Aw, Mel. I forgot my phone last night. I went out for a while then came back. I crashed out. Where you, hon?

Metropolis.

Where?

Illinois. But I'm looking across at Kentucky.

I thought you—?

You ever done that, Mo? Just stand in one state and look across at another? Maybe even have two feet in different states at one time?

Good lord, no, Mel—

Well, it's kinda neat. And it's Metropolis. There's a Superman statue here.

Sounds about right, she said.

Anyway, I never did it before just yesterday. I'm doin' it again this morning. It's like a theme for this trip.

What is?

Just to stand lookin' at two states. Just taking a minute to be. Thinking about how things can change so fast over just a short distance. Wondering about the point of all these divides and property lines in the world.

You sound punch drunk, hon.

I'm fine. Just not much sleep.

You still got any of the money I left you?

Yeah, I got money.

The car okay?

It's fine. Drives great. I like all the music you left in there.

Then what's up? You don't sound like you, hon.

I'm all right. Just no sleep. Far, too.

Well, girl, you are far. I ain't never been over that way. Heard about it. That casino hotel and all?

Yeah.

Like Tunica?

Sorta. Yeah.

You get a nice room? Treat yourself?

They were all out. Sold out, I mean.

Why didn't you keep on?

Well, I did. Sort of.

I paused.

Maureen?

Yeah, Mel?

You remember when we were kids, maybe second grade?

Yeah.

Well, you remember how we'd fight so much?

Yeah.

And how when I was so much smaller than you, and I'd finally had enough one day. I took a chain to the back of your bare legs?

Well, yeah. I had my back turned.

And how when you were down on the ground you said you'd never forgive me? You were all buckled down, screaming bloody murder? Screamin' how you'd never speak to me again?

Of course. How could I forget it?

And how a week or so later Becky Strickland pushed me right off the monkey bars and my chin split open on the top rung?

Yeah, Mel.

And how I fell backward and the blood ran down my neck and through my hair, and how she stood over me with both legs on each side of my chest?

Yeah, Mel. What is all this about?

I still think just to see me bleed? Just to have some power over me?

Well, yeah.

And how you took Becky out with a kidney punch right there?

Uh huh.

Well, for a whole life now, you been stickin' up for me. Sometimes when I feel like the whole damn world is standin' over me just like Becky did that day and I can barely catch my breath, you're always there.

Mel, that's what sisters do.

It's not what all sisters do.

Well, it's what we d—

Sometimes it takes gettin' out in the wind to see what you take for granted, how to appreciate things in a new way.

I went back over to my bench and sat down. I could hear Maureen move the receiver around some, switching ears. I heard her flick a lighter, lighting the day's first cigarette. She inhaled and blew that first drag out. There was always a rhythm in the way she did it.

Now, Melinda . . .

Maureen?

Yeah, Mel.

It's been a good few days out here in the world.

Good. I'm glad—

Like always, you gave me a gift.

Well, you already seen some places I ain't.

But I think I wanna come home now.

Parker

The belt sander arrived Thursday evening just before Ben came down. I'd found it through the classifieds in our paper, and a couple named Floyd and Carol Ann Crawford drove it over from Dyersburg in a rusted-out, white Ford dually. Floyd pulled into the driveway, hopped out, and left the truck running. He pulled a cigarette from a smashed-up pack of Basics in his T-shirt pocket and lit it up. He was a fireplug of a man with a salt-and-pepper hair comb-over and a few days' stubble. His glasses were thick, scratched, and sat crooked, and his once-white T-shirt had faded brown stains around the neck. He hiked up his navy work pants several times as he walked around the truck, popped down the tailgate and untied the two thin ropes he had holding the sander in place. The white crescent of his belly hung out of the bottom of his shirt, and he smelled like smoke and body odor. As he maneuvered around, he complained about his back, then about some asshole cutting him off on the south bypass, then he made a joke about folks east of the Mississippi. Then he yelled what? toward the cab. Then he said let me do the talkin', Carol Ann. Then he said yeah, we'll eat after this, Carol Ann. Then he said it'll only be a few minutes, Carol Ann. He came back around the truck, took a long drag off his cigarette, looked over my shoulder into the garage and said 'that where you want this thing?

He struggled getting up in the bed of the truck. When he hoisted himself onto the tailgate it was hard not to notice how about a third of his ass made its way out of the top of his pants. He crawled toward the cab, then got down behind the sander and pushed it toward the tailgate. It slid well along the ridges of the bed liner. The thing wasn't all that heavy but it was odd-shaped and cumbersome for him to maneuver. He got it toward the edge of the tailgate, then hopped down from the bed. Another waft of his B.O. hit me, and he went on about how this thing had been so good to him. Just bills to pay, he said. He lifted it and waddled it over to my workbench in the center of the garage. No sooner than we'd gotten it settled, Floyd asked for the cash. I got the roll of two hundred-fifty out of my front pocket, handed it to him, and he counted it down. I figured the pay might cheer Floyd up, but it didn't. He looked back at Carol Ann, then back at me.

Any good places to eat supper 'round here? he asked.

Maybe the Grecian if it's not too crowded. Or the catfish place out on 84 East. It'll put you back in the direction of Dyersburg, I said.

All right, he said ambling himself back up into the dually.

He backed over a good part of the yard with his rear right tire, then put it in drive. As they pulled away the truck left a cloud of black smoke hanging over the street. It hung there for a few minutes, surrounded by the late evening blue light.

Up until now I'd been sanding down old chairs and tables with basic tools. I'd taken to it occasionally on weekends, and it quickly became more about the motion and the movement than building something spectacular. It was more about that than building much of anything at all. I found therapy in it, and a route away from my fits. Or at least around them. I'd find the old chairs for cheap, work on them, then either give them away to friends or sell them for cheap. Lately I'd made small end tables. I gave Leon one and he seemed to like it. He encouraged me to keep going, and I figured the sander would help me get better and faster at it.

Ben was sleeping late, and it looked like I had a most of a Sunday ahead of me to play with. I'd used a sander before but not this particular model. I took a few minutes to get familiar with the locking system, the varied speeds of the belt, and how this particular miter gauge worked. Floyd had dinged it up some, but by and large it ran smooth. I grabbed a couple scrap pieces of wood from out back just to experiment for a little while. I smoothed the side of a small segment of two-by-four, then worked with a piece of four-by-four for a little while. I rounded the corners some, then smoothed over the edges, just to get a feel for the belt and its abilities. I took my gloves off and felt the new smoothness of wood that was out by the trash a little while ago. Just the sound of the thing brought on some new sense of possibility.

Maureen

I grabbed a twenty off the nightstand and walked down to the Flash Market. The day was heating up fast, and the town was quiet, everyone hiding out by their air conditioners. I walked in and Jimmy Ross was at the register. He was thin as a rail, pale, and wore a faded black Flash Market T-shirt. He'd worked here since we were all seniors in school, and I guessed I'd known Jimmy since around then, though never all that well.

Jimmy leaned over the counter, leafing through a gun magazine he'd probably pulled from the rack by the door. He had a patch over his left eye from a three-wheeler accident when he was fifteen. Word was that he was trying to show off for some friends out on Ronnie Baker's uncle's farm north of town. They were taking turns jumping the thing off a small dirt berm, seeing how high they could get on it. Jimmy went up, but the story was that he rose from the seat and separated from the three-wheeler, mid-air. The last part of the story was when he came down his head hit the handle bars, and the left brake lever went right into his left eye socket. No helmet. No visor. Happened just like that.

Hey Jimmy, I said.

He never looked up from his magazine.

I grabbed the one broken basket by the door, picked out some half and half, a liter of Coke, a single sleeve of Ritz Crackers, some cheddar cheese and a bottle of Yellow Tail chardonnay. I figured the twenty could cover all that.

I laid it out on the counter and he closed up his magazine.

What's up, Jimmy?

Inwardly debating milliradians versus MOA, he said.

MO what?

Minute of angle.

What's all that about? I asked, getting the twenty out of my jeans pocket.

It's about an endless debate as to which is the best angular unit of measurement, he drawled, starting to scan my items.

Why's it have to be debated? Doesn't that stuff always boil down to the skill of the shooter? I mean, the success? I said.

More or less, he said, uninterested and dulled. Each argument leads to the same answer, basically. He flipped his hands out, then scanned the crackers and the cheese.

But what else am I gonna do around here? he panned around the store. He seemed about half present. He was always this way, at least with me.

Got your I.D., Maureen?

I.D.? I felt the outside of my jeans pockets.

Shit, Jimmy. No. Left it back at the house.

Need your I.D. for the wine.

Really?

Yeah.

Why now?

Law, he said, flat.

But you've known me since ninth grade. I buy wine here all the time. Y'all haven't carded me here in years. Why now?

Law.

Now?

Not just now. That law's been in effect for a long time now.

But why are you suddenly abiding by it? I asked, annoyed.

Just need to see your I.D. for this wine.

It's at the house.

Cool, I'll hold onto it for you.

You mean you want me to walk the half mile all the way back to the house to get you an I.D. you've long known I'm good for?

Basically, yeah.

Why?

I don't know. Just feel like it today I guess. And y'know, law.

Why do you just feel like it? I felt around my jeans pockets again. Empty.

I guess 'cause the other day I decided I was sore at you again.

Sore at me again?

Yeah.

What all caused that, Jimmy?

I don't really feel like you went to bat for my sister.

Went to bat?

On that loan a while back.

The loan on the Honda?

Yeah.

The loan. Literally from years ago?

Uh huh.

That's what this is about?

Well, that, and y'know, the law.

Why now? Why're you suddenly picking this battle now?

My sister reminded me the other day. And I'm workin' through some things. Addressing issues with people of my past.

What? Why?

Helps clear my conscience.

So all this is about getting leverage back on me?

That, and the law.

Jimmy, Carla called and explained it all to your sister anyway. Told her why we couldn't do the loan.

Eh, it felt too fast.

What was too fast?

The turnaround on it. I mean, did you really try for my sister?

Of course, but I never made—

It's long been hard for me to feel like you really tried, he said, peering at me with his one visible dark brown eye.

You don't feel like I tried? I said, stunned.

191

We were just an afterthought is our guess, he said.

Jimmy, I didn't dole out the loans. I never had that power there and never made those decisions. Maybe you never knew that, or forgot or—

You should try showing some respect to folks in life. It'll get you further down the line. He flipped his hands out again.

I searched for the words. My forehead overheated. I couldn't believe it.

Anyway, I'll need to see some I.D., Maureen, he said.

Fuck this place, was all I could get out.

I grabbed my twenty off the counter. The Flash Market door dinged as Bo Brooks walked in to pay for the diesel on his old-ass, brown Cadillac El Dorado. I pushed my way past him, leaving all my items on the counter in front of Jimmy.

Hey, Maureen, Bo said.

Hey, fuck this place, Bo, I said.

I headed straight back to the house in the pitched heat.

I packed a bag in about eight minutes.

Maureen

Mel—

Good god, friend. The ghosts we run from. Then run back into again. Angry and empty. Do they ever really change? Same streets. Same feelings.

Before supper last night I stopped downtown. I held a picture of you and me in my hand. It was from when you were about eleven, I guess. Woulda made me thirteen. I stood in the spot where it was taken, held it up in my left hand, and took in the current shell of this place. Everything's closed and gone, mostly. But was anything crucial ever really here? If so, how much, and what all did it really mean? If we woulda zoomed out of our little world would it have mattered much in the first place? Maybe it would have mattered just as much.

Maybe it's just the further away we get, the more we romanticize. I'm guilty as anyone.

County still doesn't even have a proper hospital.

Yours and my America. Bury it.

But you and me managed here and there, yeah? All the way back. Took care of each other pretty well. I know I can live with that.

Leaving most everything of mine. At least for now. As always, what's mine is yours, hon. Indefinite loan. Definite loan. Whichever. House, too. Move on in to my room. Give Ben yours. He's gold, Melinda. I know you'll love him through it all. Spare nothing for a good son.

Money enclosed here for the first round of utility bills.

Car should be fine for a while. Oil change soon, registration in October. Don't forget those kinds of things and it'll take care of you.

The good fight is still ours. I'll always believe that.

I love you endless.

But I may be a while.

—Mo

I put the note and the cash in an envelope and taped it to the kitchen sink faucet. It was all I figured Melinda needed to know. It wasn't much more than I knew for the time being. I sent a text saying to let herself in when she got back to town, that I'd leave a key. She texted back a quick "k" with no punctuation. Like she was probably driving.

Maureen

I put my shoes on and looked over at my bag on the couch. I thought about the realities of hitching in this world. Mama and Daddy'd done it, but that'd been forty years back and it was a different thing then. Maybe there were just as many monsters in the world even then, but more people did it. And here I was about to strike out and take my chance. I didn't know where I'd wind up by nightfall. I only knew I wasn't hanging around here anymore. I went to the kitchen drawer and rummaged through it. I grabbed a serrated steak knife and zipped it up in the outer pocket of my bag. Just in case. I wondered if Mama and Daddy'd carried protection when they hitched. They'd never said. I locked the house up, threw the key under the backdoor mat, and started walking south down my street toward Highway 25.

Melinda

I walked the river trail back toward the Harrah's. A barge moved slowly, going the opposite way over on the Kentucky side of the river, and as the morning pushed onward, the clouds hung around, ganging up like they were gonna become something severe. A few small raindrops hit my head, and two Flycatchers circled and fluttered around a green-backed Heron about fifty yards down. Vines hung from the high trees above, and patches of poison ivy and rotted out river trash skirted the trail. I made my way up the hill toward the main parking lot, and noticed the cars had already thinned out a good bit since last night. I looked across the plane of the lot at the hole where my motel room wall used to be. The flowered curtains blew outward from the room, still suspended on a bent rod. There was a line of yellow police tape strung across it, and I could see two stocky Mexican men in orange vests at the scene, starting to clean up the debris on the sidewalk. I wrangled Maureen's car keys out of my front right pocket.

I drove up the main street where the street fair had been. All the tents were gone, and other than the sidewalk trash cans packed beyond capacity, it was as if it had never happened. I slowed past the Superman statue again, then headed out toward Highway 45. The clouds hung heavy like a charcoal wall to the west, and the sun hung brighter and heavier behind me from the east. I thought how I'd love for Ben to see that river and that Superman statue. Then I thought of about a hundred other places I'd like to take him before I took him to this one.

Parker

Need to call Leon this afternoon. He left me a message late last night and it didn't sound good. Lizzie was still in Memphis. He was headed down there for a couple days, then planned to come back, hopefully with her by mid-week.

I cut and smoothed over four pieces that would be legs for a small end table. Cedar this time. I got them to where I was happy, then moved on to what would be the tabletop. Wind blew into the garage and kicked the dust around some. A storm front was moving in over the county and I'd guessed these were the straight-line winds on the front edge. Ben was still sleeping inside. I flipped my goggles back down and got the sander going.

I worked over the top edges of the table top. I was able to create a roundness to them that I liked, and it felt effortless in the wake of doing this kind of stuff manually for so long. I wondered about Floyd and Carol Ann. I hoped they'd made it back safe, and thought about what their lives in Dyersburg might be like.

He sure was gruff. Wondered if he'd always been that way or if something'd just turned him. Broken him, even.

A long time ago, sitting at The Lantern I remember Leon said a single moment can really break a man. He said sometimes that was all it took. I argued with him that I thought it was a combination of small moments — more a sum of things. I argued that a lot of small moments can add up in a positive way, too. Those things can take from someone, but they can make someone, too. I remember around that time I asked Leon if someone handed him a piece of paper with his death date on it, would he look at it? It was something we all used to debate as kids and for whatever reason it popped back into my then-drunk head. He said not at all. He didn't wanna know. He said he wanted things to play out in their natural ways — that he wouldn't wanna live knowing something like that. I said I would. I'd like to know how much time I've got left just to figure all the things I need to do and say before I check out. He said how could you live with that? Knowing how many days you had? I said it's a big picture kind of thing, and that I'd just like to leave as few things undone as possible. I'd like to say all I want to say to my friends, family, even enemies, then die knowing I'd done all I could do to have a complete and satisfying life. He said what about the clock? He said that ticking would sure get loud toward the end. I said I could be wrong, but I don't think I'd be afraid of the clock. Especially if it turned out to be an illness that I knew was leading me to the end. I'd go out and give my hugs and speak my peace, and fly right on in to the next realm. He laughed a big belly laugh and shook his head at me. He took a drink of his beer and looked up at the TV. Then he yelled, Hey, Jerris, come over here! Jerris was washing glasses and grunted. Then Leon said Jerris, I'm serious — you need to weigh in on this heap, letting out another big belly laugh.

Rachel

At the meeting my mind drifted. Parker wasn't there again. We hadn't talked in nearly a week, and I knew he'd been spending time with his son. As folks were going around the circle, talking about their own stories, my mind started to drift. A girl named Leah Joe Watson talked, then a guy named Jerry started going on and on about how he'd hit rock bottom. I'd seen Jerry at these meetings for months but he never talked. I don't remember him speaking to anyone. He'd duck in right at the start, get a coffee, sit and listen, then leave immediately. He was barrel-chested and had jet-black hair. He wore a button-down shirt that was too big for him, paint-stained jeans and brown work boots. On this night he finally spoke. He talked about how not long ago he didn't have a thing left and how he was living out east of town along the edge of a soybean field. He said the reason he stayed out there was because he kept getting run out of places in town. Either by the cops or business owners, or high school kids that just wanted to mess with him. He said he'd tried about everywhere. Behind the Presbyterian church, in the circle of shrubs in front of the city park, under the high school football stadium bleachers, and even in the stairwell of the Super 8. In the day he'd hitch rides or walk around to try and find handouts and food, or maybe get hired for day labor in the fields. He'd spend whatever money he'd gathered through the day on liquor, slink back to the edge of the field and drink to keep warm on cold nights. To ease his mind. He went on, saying he most often slept in a dug-out hole lined with three old sleeping bags. He talked about how a few years ago he'd prostituted himself at the Love's over near Hayti on 55, just for those mini bottles of whiskey you can get up front at the counter. Said they eventually ran him off there, too. I looked up at the clock and thought about what all he'd levied on those around him, and then what the world had levied on him. I wondered if he had anyone left.

These days the one I worried about most was Ben. Things with Parker were slowing down, and I wasn't gonna come around anymore if it wasn't something we couldn't nurture. If we couldn't make something together, I wasn't gonna try to push things further. As Jerry talked, I realized it was time to let Parker know that. I didn't want us to keep sneaking around town at the expense of his son. Or his son's mama for that matter. She had a boy to think about, and as far as I could tell, some serious waters to navigate on her own. They had to share Ben and I never figured that could be easy. A few years ago I wouldn't have cared. A few years ago I would have said hell with her or anyone else. I would have said I'm gonna take whatever I want because I'm due some kind of joy from this world. But these meetings every week, they always draw a plumb line from folks' actions to their consequences. Jerry went on about how he fought out most of last winter on the edge of that field. He battled through tears and scooted up on the edge of his seat, and then he looked down at his ragged brown boots. He talked about how these meetings saved his life and how he'd slowly gotten himself back on track. He talked about how he had an apartment now and had gotten more consistent temp work around town. I took a deep breath listening to the end of his story, then looked back up at the clock. Leah Joe raised her hand like she wanted to talk again. That was when I picked up my purse and moved toward the door.

Ben

It was only a wall away.
It sounded like dad had a handle on it.
I hoped he was happy with it.
I rolled back over.
The cool air from the fan hit my feet.
Not too long before school starts.
Back to Maureen's tomorrow.
Or maybe the next day.
Maybe I could take the truck up.
I rolled back over.
Wedged my shoulder between the bed and the wall.
Fell into a half sleep.
Thought about Mama's voice.
On the phone yesterday.
Where she might be right now.
The summer I was seven, I played Little League.
Ball came real fast up the line.
Coach had me at third.
I liked second.
Coach said you'll play third.

Runner from second coming my way.
I froze up just off the base.
I moved back.
Runner from second getting closer.
Coach yelled.
Then I charged.
Coach yelled.
Runner from second real close now.
Ball popped up off a rock.
Or maybe trash or glass.
Like a laser to my left eye.
Coach yelled.
Half blackness.
Runner rounded third.
I wanna help the team.
I wanna get up.
Ball's just right there.
Coach yelled the ball's just right there!
Runner crosses home.
Ump Grant yells time.
Coach yells get the ball, Ben.
Ump Grant yells Y'all hold up!
Ump Grant runs up the third base line.
I wanna get up.
Ump Grant yells He got a parent here?!
Coach yells again.
Still half blackness.
Closed my eyes.
Laid my head back.
Opened my eyes a little.
Ump Grant says Y'all don't crowd around, boys.
Closed my eyes again.
Coach went quiet.
I heard Mama above.
Calm voice.
Smelled her hair.
Felt her strong arms.
Picked me up.

Took me away.
I was bigger now.
Hard on her back.
She carried me anyway.
Straight to the car.
Away from a tough thing.
Still does.
Most all the time.

Parker

I smoothed over the corner piece to the little table I was working on. The wind picked up outside, blowing a stream of cut grass and leaves into the garage. I turned back to work on the table, and then I thought about the guy. Melinda's new guy. Chad, Ben had said. Soldier. Could cook. Probably knew his way around a belt sander. Probably never had a problem in front of people when he was out fishing either.

I dug in along the stretches some. I wondered what he'd seen in Afghanistan. Wondered what he'd been through and what stories he told Melinda and Ben. Then I wondered how they reacted. I wondered if they were impressed and if they had a lot of questions. I bet he answered them with confidence, probably always with a good story to follow. Heroic endings. Strong forearms and a hard jawline and an assured smile with appealing dimples. Ben didn't say much more about Chad beyond what he'd told me at lunch that day. I wondered if he liked him and was afraid to play him up too much to me. Or maybe he didn't like him and just didn't wanna talk about it. If they wanted to see each other, did Melinda and him hang around his place? Or did Maureen just let them have their time at her place? I wondered what kind of fun they had up in Clarkton, and when I thought about that I just felt sour toward it all. My face felt hot and I was mad. Mad at something I couldn't see, about someone I didn't know much about. Mad in a way to where I didn't feel like I could tell anyone.

The wind whipped up outside again, and I sanded a straight section. I dug in a little more, but I got too aggressive on the belt and created a bevel along the edge. I'd have to go back and try to smooth that out, or even the rest out to match it. I put that piece down and grabbed another. Then I flipped up my goggles, grabbed a scrap piece of the floor and threw it at the wall as hard as I could. The sander kept humming. More leaves blew into the garage. I walked in a small circle for a minute and looked over at the wall. I'd put a four- or five-inch-wide dent in the sheetrock by the door. I'd have to explain that, unless maybe I could find something real quick to hang over it. Maybe a picture or a poster or something.

A car door slammed out on the street. I couldn't see the car or who it was. I moved toward the garage door and the breeze from outside hit me. It was Rachel. I'd just thrown a hole in the wall over something she had no idea about. I couldn't think of how to shift gears to start talking to her. I couldn't think of much of anything. The only thing I could think is that I knew I didn't want her to see me like this. She may not even notice but I didn't want her to see the hole or the piece of wood on the floor beneath it. I gave off half a smile as she walked up the driveway. I took off my goggles and tried to look like everything was cool. Then I took off my work gloves and shoved them in my back pocket as she walked up the driveway. I looked up to see that the skies had gotten darker, then back at her. She looked great. She had on a dark green blouse and a black skirt. It was the same black skirt she'd worn when we last saw each other. In the parking lot. I thought about how one of the most striking things about her had always been her hair. It blew across her face and over her almond eyes. She pushed it out of the way with her left hand and paused a few feet from me just inside the garage door.

Hey, she said.

I was still covered in dust and wood particles. I didn't say anything. I just formed another half-smile and waved, weak-like.

What's all this? she asked.

I moved to the side a little, looking back into the garage.

This? I got a belt sander from a guy over in Dyersburg.

You stepping up the operation?

Yeah, I just thought I would try and have a more serious go at it.

When'd you get it?

Thursday. You shoulda seen the guy that brought it, I said, trying to shift focus to other dysfunction.

Really?

Yeah. His wife just sat in the truck, and he was kind of a mess.

I was nervous. Filling space with small talk and deep breaths, trying to keep things moving.

A mess? she said.

Yeah, he had rough B.O. and didn't have much nice to say about anything or anyone. He was frazzled and in a rush and didn't call to tell me when he was arriving. All he left me with was sometime Thursday P.M.

Well, what's the matter with that? she asked.

What do you mean?

What's the matter with not calling?

Well, it's just that it'd have been nice of him to let me know when he might be landing and all. Just seems like common courtesy, I said.

You're the police of common courtesy now? she asked.

And here we went, I thought.

Well, I—

That's funny, considering how you bailed on me the other day? she said.

The other—?

When we were on the phone?

On the—?

When y'all were fishing. Did you forget?

I don't—

I don't understand why you're all upset with this belt sander guy you don't even know for not calling. You ever consider how not calling might fly with folks you're involved with? Ever consider how not calling the people that actually give a damn about you might go over?

I paused.

The people that give a damn. Particularly the ones you damn sure make time to fuck in the back of a car when it's convenient for you?

The wind whipped up again and I felt a line of sweat right at the edge of my hairline. It nestled with the first centimeters of skin on my forehead, and that all matched the cold sweat starting up at the base of my neck.

Rachel, I—

I'm all ears, Parker. Dazzle me, she said.

I heard the utility room door open behind me. I turned and saw Ben, half leaning into the garage. Sleepy-headed and half there, he surveyed both of us, then closed the door. I turned back to Rachel.

I had a rough week, I said.

How would I know anything about that? she asked.

I can't blame you if you're mad, I said.

A "rough week" doesn't tell me anything, she said sternly, using her fingers as quotation marks. What I know is that when we were on the phone the other day, when y'all were fishing, you bailed on me.

I bailed?

You bailed. We were talking, there was a mess of noise, and you were gone. And you never called back.

I paused.

Well, what went on? she asked.

I had a fit, Rachel.

You had a fit? she asked, obviously not believing me. Or not understanding.

I took a breath and felt more sweat take life along the small of my back. The sky outside darkened more and the afternoon's first rain pellets cranked up.

A fit? she said, more irritated . . .

Yeah, I had another fit, I said. I thought I'd been out of the weeds, but I had another one, and it was big. It was in front of a bunch of people at the floodways, but most importantly and I would say most unfortunately, it was in front of my son. Since then I've been walking dead, Rachel. I've been ashamed. I've been scared and I've been nervous and I don't wanna face Ben, or you, or Ben's mama, or even Leon right now. And at best . . . at my very best, I've been minute to minute, with days measured out in baby steps just trying to lose myself in building these things. These small, wooden things that could be loved just as easily as they could be thrown away. The belt sander guy doesn't know that he brought me some new portal toward focus. He doesn't know that he delivered therapy to someone struggling. I keep sanding these things, not for the end picture, but for the small moments each piece gives me.

I looked over Rachel's face. The wind blew in again and she pushed strands of clean, weightless hair out of her eyes. She opened her mouth to say something, then stopped short. That was the moment I realized it's all one big movement, laced with some hope that I'll find some evident slope of sense, and that I'll land on some sand bar of balance for my fool brain and the heartless, unpredictable sludge that's been racketing around in there for what feels like all time.

The rain started to come down heavier.

I didn't know what else to do but ask her to come on in. I was still nervous, and now I was short of breath from all I'd just thrown on her. She pulled me toward her. She hooked her arms under mine and moved her hands around my lower back. I felt her warm breath and smelled her perfume, and both were like some womb of solace after a long storm. She kissed me long on the cheek, and then unhooked her arms from around my back. She turned and headed out into the thick of the rain, uncaring of getting wet. She pulled her keys from her purse, got in the car and turned the engine over. She started down the street, then stopped at the corner for a good two minutes. She just sat there at the stop sign with the car running. Then she turned her signal on and took a left to who knows where.

Melinda

Highway 45 routed me back out into a mix of forest to the west and fields to the east. I retraced some of my steps from yesterday, passing through the town of Mermet, then two different nature preserves saw me back through Karnak. I thought about what all I'd experienced in just a day or so. I thought about the kindness of Layton and Vonda, and I felt confident in thinking how I'd probably remember them for all my life. I thought about Raylene and drunk Martin and little Opal. I wondered who she'd grow up to be in this hard, strange world. I thought about the couple at the check-in desk at the Harrah's. I'd seen meanness like that back home, from people around town that I'd known all my life were assholes. But not out in the world, and not in a way that they felt the least bit of remorse for. Not in what was supposed to be a nice place — a place where people were eating and drinking and gambling, supposedly enjoying themselves for the weekend. Rich assholes. Seen 'em on TV, but this was a first in person. I thought about how I'd never tasted gar or had a car back into my hotel room and smash it all apart. I'd never slept on a bench by a river. But I had now. Some unexpected, small life lived within a bigger life, just a state or so away. All these things and moments, souvenirs in their ways.

I wanted to stop in Karnak and say hi to Layton, but when I drove by the gas station the mean girl's beat-up Sentra was out front. It was probably her shift, and it felt strange to me that even though I was so far from home, I was already taking note of folks' patterns and comings and goings out here. I sure wanted to thank Layton again. Maybe I'd see him another day.

I missed my son. The clouds that hung to the west started to spit rain, and I held my eyes on the road and shuffled through the CDs in the passenger seat, holding each one up before me until I found what I wanted. I put in the one with Emmylou Harris Sharpied on it. A song called Where Will I Be carried me by and around and through fields of corn and cotton and soybeans. I connected with Interstate 57 near Olmsted, and it felt like it carried me at warp speed compared to those state highways. Big trucks sped around me, likely headed to Memphis and beyond from points north, and it wasn't long before I passed Mound City, Urbandale, and eventually the Big River. I wanted to look down and take in all its mystery again. I'd been around this area all my life and I still couldn't believe what a wonderful and mystifying thing it was. An element or force unto itself, wearing all the masks between beauty and fatal danger, connecting all kinds of people, cultures, trades, species, and generations.

The river flats spread below, and a big sign was suspended in the upper supports of the bridge welcoming all passers into Missouri. I needed gas soon. The rain kept on, but contrary to the darkness of the clouds, it never got too heavy. It followed me along to where I turned off on I-55 south, and as I looked over the fields south of Sikeston, I imagined that it was the kind of late summer wash most of the farmers around here were happy to get. I pulled off at a Chevron just north of New Madrid to fill the car up. I went inside to give the girl a twenty. She was thin with light eyes and blonde hair, wore a brown apron and had a rose tattoo on her left forearm. There were some initials flanking each side of the rose, and even though it was early yet she looked like she'd had a full day. The man in line in front of me was as thin and blonde as she was, and they looked almost like they could be related. He was in a navy Dickies jumpsuit, and as I walked up he was going on and on to her about something called the New Madrid Seismic Zone.

It's just a damn field, he said.

It's probably all on the internet, the girl said, counting off and plucking three Quick Picks from the roll for the man.

The seismic zone? the man asked.

No, just the information about it.

I guess I was given the wrong info on the site.

I guess you were, she mumbled.

So there's not anything more than what I described to you? Anything more around town or in the county?

No. What'd you think it'd be? she asked.

I just thought there'd be markers to with regard to the 1811 quake, and maybe . . .

You think they'd commemorate that? the girl asked smugly.

Of course! It was a major geological occurrence. That and . . .

There was widespread death and catastrophic damage, she interrupted. Hell, the river switched directions. Why should we commemorate that?

I shifted my hips and settled in now. I grabbed two Heath bars and a pack of Skittles from the three-for-three bin.

I just think with a major historical occurrence like that . . . one of the largest fault lines in the world and all, right here, with something called the New Madrid Seismic Zone there'd be plenty of—

Marketing opportunities? she interrupted.

Maybe you got a joke played on you, she said.

What? he said.

You want coffee mugs and T-shirts? A bounce house? she asked, scratching her tattooed arm. She started to wilt him with the stare of a long-disappointed mother.

I'd think with a fault line like this . . . Aw, nevermind he said, tangled in his argument. He slammed the exact change for the Quick Picks down on the counter and stormed out of the store toward a white, long-used Dodge panel van.

Not my fuckin' fault, she muttered downward, then laughed low.

I stepped up and put my candy down on the counter. I rummaged around my right pocket for some cash. I still had the three hundred from Raylene, but the envelope from Maureen felt pretty thin. I pulled it out and saw that there was thirty bucks left in it.

What you need, girl? She took a deep breath, asking with a new tone of voice. She gave off a sympathetic smile.

Just these and twenty of unleaded on four.

Twenty-three twenty-five, she said.

I handed her the thirty bucks and she gave me back the change.

The store had cleared out from a small morning rush, and the jumpsuit man was pulling out of the parking lot in his beat-up van.

Bet you get good mileage outta that not-my-fault joke, I said, grabbing up my candy.

Once a week, she said without hesitation.

She didn't look at me when she said it. She just looked out over the parking lot. It was her world here. I could tell.

Maureen

The rain just wouldn't come, and that was all right, considering my place and time along the shoulder of 25. I looked down at my tennis shoes and wondered how much walking they'd be up for. I'd need some new ones along the way. A dark line of clouds hung toward the east end of the county and I thought about Melinda, maybe somewhere out that way. I'd been standing on the side of the highway for half an hour by the time someone picked me up. The rig was a late-model red Mack, and the trailer was old and mismatched. A faded, royal blue thing that looked like it'd been pulled from an auction yard. The driver wore a straw, tweaked-out cowboy hat like you might see on sale at the Flying J or on the singer from Poison, and an oversized red golf shirt. He had on fake black Ray-Bans and leaned over to open the passenger side door. A black lab popped its head through the bunk area curtain behind the seats.

Where you goin' hon?
   Kansas City-ish.
   Come on up!

214

Really?

Yeah I can at least get ya' to Joplin.

I said thanks and heaved my bag in the floorboard. He reached over and extended a hand to pull me up into the truck. I situated my feet around my bag, and then the reality fell on me that I'd never actually been up in a semi. It was clean and smelled like sweet lemons in the cab.

I'm Donnie. Donnie Shaw, he said. He relocated a half-empty soft pack of Winstons and a stainless steel coffee tumbler from the cup holders between us as I settled in.

I'm Maureen, I said, and shook his hand.

The lab crawled out from the bunk area and sat down between us, eager and friendly. It smelled my forearm and my shoulder and its tongue was hanging out. It seemed happy to meet someone new and I gave it a quick pet along its head and jawline.

This is Ely, Donnie said.

I kept petting the dog as if it was the only friend I had.

What you got goin' up in KC? he asked.

Friends, I said, lying.

What part of town they in?

Lee's Summit, I said, lying more.

Then I lied more and said I was looking forward to getting back up there.

The truck huffed off the shoulder and back onto 25, crawling back up to speed. A couple of northbound cars sped around us. Mama would have killed me for every bit of this. If there was ever such a thing as a visitation or a presence, she sure as shit would have come in strong as all fuck from The Beyond and wrung my neck, just as sure as I was sitting in this truck right now. But I guess there wasn't. And she didn't. And as far as I was concerned, my hot and once never-ending press of days in this little town needed to take a rest for a while. I needed not to see it and all its inhabitants for a length of time. I didn't know exactly what I wanted, but what I didn't want had been pulsating, dying a slow death right before me, and I didn't feel like I had a thing to lose on this day. I looked at Clarkton roll by beyond the passenger side window, and I thought of all the years of strange pains and joy and confusion and love and anger and sadness that I'd had there. I knew every crease and crack of this town, and it knew the same of me. Like a tired lover that can complete all your sentences, but just can't keep you. My whole life was in this little town, and here it was once more, lawns being cut and convenience store boys gossiping and summer rug rats riding bikes. Today under an overcast filter of heat and sweat and damp. All of it going by, heart barely beating on another unsuspecting, hollow summer afternoon that in time would blur itself in with all the others.

Melinda

Parker would always tell me about the times when his daddy would take him up in that plane. Back when he was a kid. His memories about it always seemed consistent and clear. He said he could tell each little town from the air, even when he was little. He could spot the St. Francis, and of course the Mississippi. He'd spy other small lakes and rivers and bark out their names. He said he could tell where one county ended and another began, and could name the names of staff people they knew at all the little airports they stopped at. He always said from up there the whole world looked like a green and gold and brown patchwork quilt. Especially in the summer when the fields were thriving. I asked him if he was ever scared to go up in that plane, and he always said no. He said his daddy was steady and calm, and always kept that little plane as maintained as the time and days would allow. I'd never been in one. Still haven't. I never told Parker outright, but I didn't ever wanna go up in one of those little planes.

I drove south toward Marston. The rain hung steady for a while, then backed off, then picked up again. After a half hour or so

I peeled off at Portageville and started west toward Clarkton. I remember Parker said his daddy would sometimes land the plane for gas in Portageville, then they'd go up toward Sikeston or even Cape on the clearest days. I wondered if Parker had anyone new hanging around. I wondered if he did, if I knew her or if I'd seen her around. And if he did, I wondered if she'd met Ben, and what Ben thought of her. If they got along. Then I wondered if all that was true, if he told her all these same stories about his daddy, them flying around, and all the things he'd always share with me. Or if maybe he got tired of going on about those things and left them all to dust over with the memory of me. Of us.

I shook myself out of it and focused back on the two-lane. I looked in the rearview mirror and one of those new Dodge Chargers was right on me. So close I couldn't even see its headlights. It was bright yellow and I could see the silhouette of a broad-shouldered, square-headed man driving. He swerved around in the lane while a semi passed us in the opposite lane. I could see him waving his arms around, like I was going too slow. Another semi passed us going the other way. He got his hands back on the wheel, then flipped his hands out in an end-of-his-rope kind of way. He was pissed off. He flashed his lights at me and swerved around in the lane a little more. The road had had me in some reverie that maybe I shouldn't have been in. Parker memories. The man finally got enough space to get around me, and when he did he glared right over at me. Then he gunned it at what must've been eighty-five or ninety. He sped off out of sight. I went ahead and sped up some, too.

It was late afternoon by the time I got to Clarkton. The streets were wet and steam was rising up off of them. Some of the neighborhood kids were playing out in the ditches and riding bikes around in all the humidity. The heat had piled up for so long by this point in the summer that most of the boys didn't even wear shirts anymore. I recognized a few of the kids when I pulled onto Maureen's street. I felt like I'd been gone so long.

Like I'd lived some small life in places they may never see, along highways they may never drive, around people they'd probably never meet. I felt like I'd been through enough to where when I saw them I waved at them like they were family. I felt happy to see them. Snaggletooth smiles and flip-flops. Cards in their spokes and temporary tattoos and bruises on their shins. I heard one of 'em yell out Oh goddamn y'all, she had her sister's ride! When I passed. Come summer these kids were the eyes and ears of the whole place.

Maureen's was quiet when I pulled into the driveway. The curtains were drawn and a bunch of promotional junk mail was jammed in the mailbox. I cut off the car. I thought about my bag back at the motel and realized other than the keys, I didn't have a thing to bring into the house. I pulled the wad of junk mail out of the mailbox and went around back. I knew she wouldn't be here when I landed, but that's about all I knew. I fished the key from under the doormat and went on in. I poured a glass of water and sat down at the kitchen island. I looked through the mail ads half-interested, and thought about the miles I'd done since I was last sitting here. I thought about what all I wanted to tell Maureen when she got in. Then I saw an envelope taped to the faucet, and for what suddenly felt like a hundred reasons all the new experiences and memories I wanted to share with Maureen flashed away, and my heart sank straight down to the pit of a godforsaken, rank, and forgotten soil beneath me and all the rest of us left here.

Maureen

You from that little town back there? Donnie asked.

Clarkton?

That was Clarkton? Where I picked you up?

Yeah.

I wasn't really payin' attention. This is a new route for me and I don't know all these towns yet.

You care if I smoke? he asked. The truck rumbled forward and the cab bounced some.

I don't, I said.

Without taking his eyes off the road he pulled a Winston from the soft pack in the cupholder, lit it up and cracked the window. Ely crawled back into the bunk area. Donnie blew the smoke from the first drag long and rubbed his chin, looking at the road.

What was your old route? I asked.

Until two weeks ago I was working further south. Jonesboro, Little Rock on down to Shreveport, sometimes El Dorado. Shorter-haul stuff through the region. A night or two gone, then home.

That's all?

Yeah. I'm semi-retired. No more winter driving across the mountain west or anything. I did that for twenty-one years. All for J.B. Hunt. I'm done with that shit. This is all catch-as-catch-can, independent contract stuff.

You do it all yourself?

No. Company called Owens Freight lines it up for me. Family operation. Went to high school with the owner. My truck, their trailers. They get a cut of course, but it's easy and I don't have to hustle no more. I work when I want, and don't work when I don't want.

He shrugged his shoulders and took another drag. The clouds were clearing some and mid-afternoon saw sunbeams streak down over Malden. The grass on the side of the highway glistened and half a rainbow made its way into view against a dark wall of clouds to the east.

Where's home? I asked.

Paragould.

So what's the new route?

Now they've got me doin' due north. I still start from Jonesboro but for instance, today I've got stops in Dexter, Poplar Bluff, then over to Joplin for my last delivery tonight. We'll probably land there around midnight. I'll bunk there and head back tomorrow.

What all are you delivering?

Just about anything. Today the Dexter stop is dropping a skid of weed trimmers to an implement and mower business up there. Then Poplar Bluff is a count of twenty-five unassembled bed frames to a furniture store. Tonight in Joplin is two skids of gaskets, pipe, and fittings to a small environmental company.

What's the weirdest stuff you delivered? I asked.

Aww, no. Don't ask.

What is it?

You don't wanna know.

C'mon.

You really wanna know?

Yep.

He took another drag off his cigarette, shook his head, blew the smoke upward and out the window, and chuckled. When he did his belly bounced some.

I don't wanna talk about it.

Say it!

I was surprised at my demand, especially directed toward this guy I didn't even know.

He looked off to the fields on his left and giggled.

Penis candles, he said.

What?!

Penis candles.

Really?

Yep.

They make those? I asked.

Well, yeah. So I found.

He flicked his ash out the window.

I can't believe it.

You wanted to know, he said, laughing again.

Before I could laugh, he went on.

Look, I gotta load all this shit in and out of the trailer. I see the paperwork and have to visit all these places. Then deal with the faces.

A bunch?

A bunch of what? he asked.

Penis candles! I yelled.

Yeah. I mean, all colors. Different lengths and shapes. Strawberry, vanilla, coconut. Amaretto, pumpkin spice. I mean, so the boxes said, he laughed.

No shit?

Yeah.

Who'd you have to deliver 'em to?

Three different stores. Not all that far from where we are right now, actually.

Do they sell?

How'm I s'posed to know? It's not like I stick around to find out.

Well, do the store people tell you anything?

Look, what I deliver is not my business. It is to an extent, but it's not. And in cases like those I gotta keep a straight face. But in my experience with this so far, more often than not, some stoned cashier kid greets me. He's gotta try to get it together, then we've gotta go through the paperwork. Then he's gotta make sure his store's got all the penis candles they ordered, 'cause if they don't, he's in trouble, see? Then if for some reason there's not enough, he's all "Hey, I'm short a couple penis candles, man." And then what?

I don't know. What? I asked.

Well, first I gotta keep a straight face. But then what am I supposed to do? Nick off the next store's box of penis candles to please him? Or does he get the full order and then I gotta deal with shorting the next store on *their* penis candles?

Well, maybe? I asked.

Okay, but if I do, then we got unhappy penis candle sellers. And then we got empty hands with regard to the area's penis candle consumers.

Well, have you had to replenish and deliver more to 'em? I asked.

I'm two weeks into this route, Maureen, he said. Your guess is as good as mine as to how the consumption of penis candles in greater Butler and Ripley counties is going to shake out over this quarter.

I can accept that, I said, looking over the highway.

Ely stuck his head out of the bunk area. I reached over to pet him and the road hummed hard beneath us. Donnie reached over and turned the radio up. Conway Twitty's You've Never Been This Far Before hit its second verse. It played out in the cab for the next couple of minutes. The fields whirred by and the song hung in the air, and that half a rainbow had almost become a full one by now.

Melinda

I put the note back in the envelope and a familiar cold shot through my armpits and all over the back of my neck. The kind you get when you walk up to the edge of a building or maybe a cliff. The kind where the safety net you thought you'd have for life is just gone from under you, and the kind where nowhere feels right. I panned around the living room. I heard all our voices and smelled Maureen's cooking and her white wine. I smelled the smoke from her cigarettes and heard the raspy laugh from deep in her lungs and saw her fumbling to wrap herself up in that old housecoat on cold nights. The way she'd stand in the doorway of her bedroom saying We'll have a time and Girl, I got you, when we'd talk about our plans and say our goodnights. There were a couple of cigarette butts in the ashtray on the island, and the faint trace of her lipstick on each one. The dish rag was still damp, draped over the kitchen sink faucet. I panned around the living room again. It didn't look like she'd taken much. I went over to the couch and the place darkened when the sun fell behind some of the late afternoon summer clouds. The neighborhood kids' voices had quieted and they'd gone in, which meant about the only company I had, even indirectly, was gone.

I fell asleep on Maureen's couch. It was the kind of sleep where my legs and chest felt like they were made of pewter. The phone rang and I bumped the keys and a ballpoint pen off the table reaching for it. Lower sun shot through the front drapes.

Hello?

When were you thinking about coming down to get Ben?

Hey, Parker.

What time works?

Ben texted and told me about the truck. Can't he drive it on up?

He can't because I've still gotta get the insurance set up for him. I figured you might be here by now at least.

What time is it?

Six-thirty.

Shit, Parker.

Where are you?

I'm sorry. I overslept this one. I just got back into—

Where are you?

Clarkton.

Can you maybe get on the road soon?

Yeah. Of course.

There's still all these houseplants of yours here. Did you want those?

Yeah, Parker. I—

I don't know how to care for them right. I feel like you should rescue 'em sooner than later.

I'll get a few when I come down. Many as Mo's car'll hold.

All right. See ya' in a while.

Tell Ben I can't wait to see him.

Sure.

Sure?

Yeah. Or you can do it when you get here.

Then a dial tone.

He still had his moments where he could cut me apart. More times than not, at least back then, it meant a fit might not be far off.

I got my shoes on and grabbed the keys. I flipped the sink and back porch lights on knowing we'd be back after dark, then locked the place up. I backed Mo's car out of the driveway and the kids were back out playing in the street. I had the driver's side window down. When I put the car into drive I heard one of one of the little girls yell Oh, goddamn, she gone again!

Then one of the little boys yelled Fuck yeah . . . girl allllways rollin'!

Maureen

Donnie made his deliveries to Dexter and Poplar Bluff. My body was tired and I drifted in and out against the window as we pulled out of Poplar Bluff. Evening came on and Highway 60 took us through Elsinore and Mountain View, on into the hills. By now Ely and I had made friends to where he had his head on my lap. I reached down and got a flannel out of my bag, then folded it up and used it as a makeshift pillow. The ditches and the pinks and oranges of the sunset gave way to half-formed sleep. In, then out, then back in again. I was half conscious when I heard Donnie roll down the window. He lit up another cigarette and I looked over with glazed eyes and pushed my hair out of my face. He kept watch over the road and broke the silence.

Maureen, you awake over there?
  Yeah. Mostly.
  We're on the outskirts of Springfield. You wanna stop and eat?
  Yeah. Mostly.
  Mostly?
  I'm hungry, I said.

I pulled my head off the window and thought about Melinda. I figured she'd be back in Clarkton by now. Maybe she'd seen my note. I'd call in a while. We pulled into the parking lot of the Springfield Flying J. Night had set in, and when I got out of Donnie's truck I could hear the engine howls of other trucks moving along I-44. I thought about how I hadn't been near an interstate in a while. Then I thought about how I hadn't been anywhere in a while. A wiry girl named Paula seated us in the Denny's. She was striated and toned, her left forearm tattooed with a blackbird flying over barbed wire. She brought us waters and a pot of coffee. It was the first time I'd seen Donnie straight on, and his face and shoulders seemed wider now. His eyes bright and blue, alive and present. A blonde wisp of hair hung out from under his stone grey Carhartt cap. He reached for two packets of sugar, held them together, tore the tops off of each, poured them into his coffee. Then he put the slivers of the tops back into the empty packets.

If they come looking for me, this'll be the trail.

Sugar packets?

The way I do 'em here. I always put the tops back into the packets. Neatly, he said, laughing.

Why?

Saves space. Literally fifty percent less cleanup for the staff.

Less cleanup?

Economy of materials. Space and time. Easier for recycling.

Is it really easier? I asked.

Saves a step. I figure if you can save a step here or there, then maybe that makes the world a little better.

You hold doors open for people?

Usually, yeah.

Hotel rooms? You leave them orderly? Put things back together?

Uh huh. I try to use just one towel, leave all the trash in the trashcan and separate the recyclables out.

What about lane changes? I asked.

Lane changes?

Well, yeah. Part of your profession.

Like when I'm passing with the rig?

Yeah.

Get back over as soon's I can, he said.

Economy of space and time again?

Yep, he said.

So what wins? Consideration for others or economy of space and time? I asked.

They're both crucial in their ways. They're connected. Contagious, I think.

You try not to waste a thing.

Well, no. I carry a lot of stuff and it takes time. So I try to think about how it affects the space around me and the people in that space.

For instance, he said, two weeks ago I was doing a small run in Arkansas. It was a four-lane highway and traffic was pretty thick along this one stretch. I was carrying a heavy load and the truck was full and slow. I was stuck in the right lane, just trying to get around a rig with an oversized load. It was literally half a house.

And? I asked.

Well, I had my signal on to pass and it took eight minutes to finally get the space to get around that rig.

Why?

People flying by. No one letting me in.

You think they were all out to get you?

No. But some folks might think that.

Then why?

Most of 'em just thinking about other things, probably. Not meaning any harm. Just minds elsewhere.

Who let you in?

An old man in an early '90s green Honda Accord.

You remember him?

I do. It was a small move on his behalf, but he could tell I was having trouble. He could tell I just wanted to get around. So he flashed his lights and let me in and gave a wave.

And here you are remembering him weeks later.

Right, Donnie said. That was all it took. He didn't know I'd been trying to pass for eight minutes, but maybe he sensed it.

I looked over the menu, then looked back at Donnie. His menu was closed and sideways under his elbows. He leaned in and took a long sip of his coffee, looking me in the eyes.

Maybe I've made too big a deal of it, Donnie said.

Why?

'cause I guess it's the way I most often see the world.

Space and time?

Yeah.

How? I asked, decided on my order and putting down the menu.

It's just stuff I consider when I'm out there. I feel like I see a lot of small missteps and cut corners in this world. Those lead to bigger ones. It's all connected. At least to me.

Even cramming tops of used sugar packets back in to save space?

Even that.

I looked over at Paula, checking on her tables, then back at Donnie.

He checked his phone.

We're doing fine, Donnie said.

We are? I asked.

Yeah.

Why?

Because Joplin texted and said there's another delivery. The dock's delayed for another half hour or so.

Paula came back, took our orders and headed off to another table.

What are you leavin' back in Clarkton? Donnie asked.

Not much. Bank job. My place. But my sister will handle the latter.

Your sister?

Yeah, she's staying there for a while. Her son's around some, too.

What brought that together? Donnie asked.

She split up with her old man a while back. So my place is a safety net in its way.

Anyone for you? Donnie asked.

No. Not really.

Why not?

There's just not.

Why?

Because it's Clarkton.

Sounds like maybe there was.

There was a guy, sort of.

Who?

Just a guy. Thing was, he was interested in my sister.

And?

Some energy.

You act on it?

For a time I worried that I would. But it came down to the wire and I shut it down.

Really?

I love my sister. I won't fuck that up.

Of course. You probably shouldn't.

And on top of that I've come to love her son, too.

Sure. I mean, I can't know exactly. But the way you've told me I feel like I know.

Donnie fiddled with his fork and napkin.

Any other energy? he asked.

Like I said, it's Clarkton. If you don't find a friend earlier on in life, odds are you just don't find a friend.

Seems that way in all those little towns, Donnie said.

What about you?

Me?

Yeah, anyone back in Paragould?

Well. Yeah.

Well? I asked.

Well, what?

What's her story?

Donnie paused and took another long sip of his coffee.

Well.

Well, what?

It's not that simple.

How's it not that simple?

It's not a her.

What?

It's not a her.

Really?

No. I mean, yeah. His name's James.

James?

Yeah.

Well?

Well. Been together a little more than two years now.

Paula came back around and topped off our coffee.

Shit, Donnie. I assumed . . .

A lot of people do. It's no big deal.

I'm sorry. I guess I just thought—

It's all right. No big deal.

How's that work? I asked.

It all works, he said wryly.

That's not what I mean.

Then what do you mean?

Well, I gotta say I don't think I ever met a gay man. Much less a gay man that's a trucker from Paragould, Arkansas.

You've probably met a gay man, Maureen.

Not to my knowledge.

Exactly, he said.

Well, how's it happen in a place like Paragould? I asked.

I don't know. How would it happen in Clarkton? he asked.

Do your coworkers know?

No.

No?

Not at all. As far as I know.

You keep it from them?

I fill out my forms and do my routes, Maureen.

You don't go out for drinks or talk about life stuff? Office parties?

I don't. The rest of the guys do, but I don't.

What about James?

Same situation.

How?

He just can't talk about it where he works.

Where's he work?

Paragould High. Assistant football coach. Algebra teacher.

My god, so y'all . . .

He's divorced. Two daughters in Jonesboro that he sees every two weeks.

He's got kids?

Yeah. Age five and three.

What about his ex?

Apparently unsurprised by all of it.

She had a hunch?

I think she knew. Which was less of a deal given that she entertained other forms of attention.

And you? When did you know?

First grade.

So no ex-wives or kids or anything?

God, no.

Donnie straightened the utensils on his napkin.

It's not like a switch flipped, Maureen. I've known who I am all my life.

He sipped his coffee.

James and me just kept it quiet.

Well, in Paragould, how do y'all . . .

We don't . . .

You don't?

I mean, we don't do anything. We usually leave town on the weekends.

Where?

Just camping or hiking somewhere. Or maybe go up to Branson or Bull Shoals. Memphis or something.

So that's the way it's been for two years running?

That's the way it's been, he said. He smiled in a way that sharpened his blue eyes. His dimples cut through his facial hair.

Paula came back around with our food and set it down. Neither of us acknowledged her this time.

What's y'all's plan for the long run?

He cut into his eggs and looked across the room, then back at me.

I don't really know, he said.

Donnie ate quietly, and suddenly the better part of me wanted to get up from my side of the booth, take my plate and go around and sit right next to him.

Parker

Fucker.
You fuck you fuck you fuck.
Bitches. You web of bitches.
These walls my terror halls.
You it.
But you ain't shit, lil bit.
You ain't shit, lil bit.
Others before.
Now you.
Fucker.
You.
You fuck.

I never heard the belt slip. I thought I had more space than I did.
I remember that I couldn't get a straight line on the fourth and
final leg for the little table. I got the first three done just right, but
the fourth just wasn't coming. Then I overcompensated and went
too far. I was in a mood after thinking of Melinda and whoever
that guy was. Then this Rachel stuff. I just couldn't stand it. I cut

too deep and that's when I slid forward. That was it. The belt caught hold of part of me. A good bit of me, and I started to go down. I saw the blur of the window on the west side of the garage, then the fluorescent light above. I remember more leaves and wind coming in as I started to fall. A white hot burned in my palm and then my left wrist. I felt the cool of the evening air on new, escaping blood, and as I fell I felt the cool metal on the sander's casing in my left palm, and then the unforgivingness of the concrete floor. Last I remember I was on my side. I screamed for Ben. I closed my eyes, and clearer still, an image of Melinda and me at our old kitchen table, right after Ben was born. Her parents had come over and we'd made them supper. Little Ben was in Melinda's arms as she ate.

So did you mean it? her dad asked. He sat slumped to his right, arm draped around the chair. He had on one of the three tattered flannel shirts he kept in rotation, no matter the time of year, and greasy brown hair combed over. He'd bounced from job to job, and always had a one-up hardship story for whoever was willing to listen.

Mean what? I asked.

To have a kid at this time.

Of course. I said, looking over at Melinda.

He chuffed like he didn't believe me.

Big responsibility, he said.

I know. That's what parenting is.

We're all right, Dad. Melinda interrupted.

Well, we all know it hasn't been easy for just you two.

Her dad prodded like this at times, particularly after he had a few beers. He never liked me and this was how he liked to showcase it. Onstage and in front of whoever was around.

We'll be ready. We are ready, I said. We're saving a little here and there.

Her dad didn't respond.

Like everyone else, I said. Then I went back to chewing.

I looked over at Ben, sleeping in his mama's arms, then up at Melinda.

We'll be fine, Melinda said.

Honey, you have to trust them. Melinda's mom said. She always tried to ease the air in the room.

Those were different times and you and I both held strong jobs. This scene don't seem like that, he said. As he said it he motioned with his left arm toward Melinda, Ben, and me. We were just some bad example to her dad now.

I pushed my chair back and excused myself. Went out for some air on the back porch. Her dad followed suit. Once he closed the door leading to the dining room he backpedaled.

Parker, I just wanna know that y'all are ready for—

We're ready, I said cutting him off. And I won't sit at my own table in front of my family and be held responsible for your short-comings and failures as a father, I said.

The wind blew through the trees above us and the last of the evening's sunset hung on in the west. I pulled a cigarette from my shirt pocket, a lighter from jeans pocket. He pulled out a cigarette from his flannel shirt pocket. He stood without a word, but clearly trying to find something to say. I lit my cigarette and then his. I walked off toward the edge of the backyard, near the line of trees and leaned against the hurricane fence, feeling a dizziness that was probably due to dehydration. Maybe stress. Then I leaned over the top of the fence and threw up all my supper.

A family of blackbirds flitted over me, singing strong and playing. They were oblivious to the situation just below, and right about then the light in the sky finally surrendered to night.

Melinda

I was trying to turn a corner with this trip. I saw it as some new experience and maybe even a fresh start once I got back, but I never considered coming home to no Maureen. I never thought I'd be the one showing up to the empty house. I never thought I'd be the one that had to let her go. I always thought I'd be the one leaving. I looked off over the soybean fields to my right. I sped the car up and went around a large John Deere tractor. Night had almost set in and the flicker of lights from our old town started to show on the horizon in the distance. All the things we'd been through under that little patch of sky. How cruel we'd been, and how much we'd laughed, cried, screamed, worked, played and fucked. Where little Ben learned to walk and dad came undone. All under that little patch of sky. Lot of sleepless nights there, but a lot of good, too. I passed another old John Deere as the town lights got closer. Mosquitoes crashed against the windshield. Fast deaths. Unknowing, then piling up with hardly a twitch. Like most of us, just trying to get through the night.

Ben

I heard that scream out there.
  Other side of my bedroom wall.
  Snapped out of my doze.
  I had a feeling.
  Had a feeling of what had happened.
  That scream.
  Wasn't like any others I'd heard from him.
  Wasn't a fit.
  I knew.
  I got up from my bed and rushed.
  Ran out of my room.
  Through the hall.
  Socks on cheap vinyl.
  Sliding in place.
  Sliding to the hallway door.
  Opened into the garage.
  Threw it open.
  Holding on to the door frame.
  And there he was.
  On his side.

Dad, no.
Please, please no.
Not like this.
Trail of new blood on the concrete floor.
Wind blew in.
I saw blood soaking his long-sleeve work shirt.
Spreading through the fabric.
Up his arm.
He groaned.
I heaved and sunk down to him.
I heaved again.
I took my hoodie off.
I wadded it up.
Put it under his neck for support.
Took my right sock off.
Got it wrapped around his wrist as best I could.
Knotted it tight.
Took my left sock off.
Got it wrapped around his palm as best I could.
Knotted that tight, too.
Need you to call Mama, he whispered.
Call Mama, he whispered again.
Ok.
She's on her way, he groaned.
But, call her, tell her faster, he said.
He closed his eyes after that.
He closed them tight and grabbed toward his wrist.
I got my phone.
I hit call.
I waited.
With it to my ear.
It rang.
I held my hand behind Dad's neck.
I felt his sweat back there.
I leaned over.
I kissed his forehead.
It rang more.
Then Mama picked up.

I heard the hum of the road beneath her on the other end of
the line.

Mama?

Ben?

Come, Mama!

What?

Need you here now, Mama.

You okay? she asked.

Need you here real soon, I said.

My voice shook at the end.

It shook and then went up.

The way a voice does at that point.

That point when the tears come on.

And they came on fast.

For the first time since.

For the first time since I couldn't remember.

Maureen

We walked across the parking lot back to the truck.

We still okay on time? I asked.

Yeah, Donnie paused.

What? I asked.

You care if I call you Mo?

No.

Not too informal?

I don't care, I said.

I been wanting to just call you Mo all day. But didn't wanna assume.

I'm okay with it.

Yeah? Donnie shoved his hands into his pockets.

Yeah. Feels good that way.

Why?

Just more familiar, I said. Endearment.

Cool. His blue eyes fell tight into a smile. Small slits of happiness.

This feels like some gift.

What?

This trip, I said.

It's a trip to you. A route to me, Donnie shot back.

But the chance of it. You picked me up. The ride today, and that sunset, and the plainness of the Denny's, and the fact that I know some things about your life in Paragould. The fact that we're here now.

The moment of you riding around with a gay trucker delivering a bunch of shit that's just gonna wind up in landfills?

Yes. I said, laughing.

Okay.

The rain from earlier had left a sheen across the parking lot. Sprinkles started to fall again, and the wind was picking up. Traffic whined louder just beyond the trees toward I-44.

You don't leave your town much, do you, Mo?

No. I said. Not much these days at least.

Why you leavin' Clarkton with no real plan? Donnie asked.

What?

You don't really have a plan, do you?

I shoved my hands deeper into my pockets. The rain started to come down a little steadier.

I have a plan.

What is it? Donnie asked.

Kansas City for now. We'll see beyond that.

We'll see? he asked.

Can't a girl just go without a plan?

I don't like it.

What don't you like about it?

I don't like the idea of just dropping you out here without you having any real plan.

Why?

It's not right, Donnie huffed.

You got a home and as far as I can tell, some family leaning on you back there.

He pulled the pack of Winstons from his shirt pocket, put one in his mouth, then extended the pack toward me.

I took one.

He lit both of our cigarettes in one move as the rain fell harder.

I'd feel a lot better if you had a plan, he said, blowing the smoke off the first drag.

It is what it is, I said, blowing the smoke off mine first, too.

That don't mean a thing.

What?

Aren't you a little bit scared?

Of what?

Of being a woman alone out in this world these days?

Why?

Have you not been paying attention?

To what?

Well, maybe to the long-running historical fact that a lot of men, famous and not so much, are constantly being exposed as long-running and chronic and horrific creeps?

Like that actor or the comedian?

Yeah, to start. Damn near every other politician, too.

Well, yeah but that's—

It's never that far. You ever consider who I could've been?

What do you mean?

Back in Clarkton. You just jumped up in my truck on trust.

I know.

You wanted out of that town so bad that the possibility of something bad happening didn't matter to you?

No. Well, not really.

I could've been some monster. I could've been or done any number of horrific things by now.

I can handle it. I can figure it out.

I like you, Mo. But I think that's horseshit.

Horseshit? I said.

Horseshit, he said.

I'm armed, Donnie.

You're armed?

I got a knife.

A knife won't do all that much in this world, Mo.

Could have cut the fuck out of you.

You need better protection, doing what you're doing. You need to think this through.

The rain started to come down steady. An older couple ran across the parking lot to get out of it and stepped into the restaurant.

Why do I have to live like that?

Secure?

Scared? I said.

It's just a matter of security, Mo.

I don't have to walk through this world like that.

Secure?

Scared, Donnie. I'm talking about the constant selling of fear. I won't buy into it. If I'm meant to go, then I'm meant to go.

Why?

Call it a line cast into the pond of chance. I said.

It is what it is to you? Donnie said.

It is what it is.

That statement's worthless to me, he said.

Why?

It says nothing. And don't tell me that you'll figure it out, he said making quotation marks with his fingers.

Why, I asked. My voice was raising, now in sheets of pouring rain. We were both fully soaked and the white noise of water on pavement was mounting.

That's just nonsense folks say on the loading dock to fill space. Shit they say when they're not creative enough to dissect their thoughts or thoughtfully assess a situation. Or when they're just nervous. Those things just fill the air. They don't mean anything, Mo.

What'm I supposed to say then, Donnie?

You're not supposed to say anything right now, Mo.

Why?

Because I don't know. Because I don't wanna talk about it anymore.

You don't wanna talk?

I don't. What I want is for you to look carefully at both of us right now, soaked to the bone in this godforsaken Joplin parking lot, arguing over this shit.

Donnie smiled when he said it.

I started to smile, too.

We broke into a short laugh on account that maybe there was a silliness to it all.

Donnie's laugh fell away. He looked down and then back up at me.

What I want you to do is get a full load of this tired human in front of you, he said. Look at the bags under my eyes. All this mess. He drew his arms outward slowly, waving them in a ballet kind of way.

His eyes fell open. He looked vulnerable. For the first time in any of this, Donnie looked uncertain.

He slowly sat down on the yellow curb in front of us.

And then what I want you to do, Mo, is just sit with me for a minute. Don't say a goddamn 'nother thing. Just sit with me and watch this rain.

I sat down by his side and turned my head toward him.

Tears filled Donnie's eyes. I turned and hooked my arms under his. The rain kept on, watering us to our cores. By now my chin was on Donnie's shoulder. The smell of what seemed like years of cigarettes was embedded in his vest. I looked over the parking lot wondering what my next move really was, and in the distance I heard a woman's voice over the Flying J P.A. system announce that shower number three was ready.

Melinda

I rounded the corner, and from down the street I could see the light spilling from the garage onto the driveway. As I got closer I saw Ben pacing with his phone in his hand, palm aglow. I parked crossways in the driveway, got out and ran toward Ben. Just behind I saw Parker on the floor under the new sander. A wide stream of blood crossed the concrete floor between him and Ben. Ben was frozen, hyperventilating, and now leaning against the garage doorframe. He'd muttered the word "ambulance" softly, and I could already hear the siren in the distance. He tried to say something else, but I moved beyond him and down to Parker. I tightened the socks around Parker's wrist and palm. They were each saturated with blood to where they slipped when I pulled the ends. I turned back and saw Ben leaned against the doorframe. He was doubled over now. A stream of vomit rained out of his mouth to the garage floor . . . I raised back up, ran into the house, down the hall to the bathroom, and grabbed two hand towels out of the cabinet. I ran back to the garage and pulled the bloody socks off Parker's palm and wrist. I folded one hand towel long ways and tightened it around his wrist, trying to distribute the pressure just right, then did the same with the second one. The

siren got closer. The whir of the sander still filled the garage and
I flipped it off. I checked Parker's breathing and it seemed stable.
He moaned an awful tenor mess of sound and opened his eyes up
to me.

Heyy, he groaned.
    Save your energy, Parker. Just let me work on this.
    I tightened the towels, then checked pulse on his neck and wrist.
He sighed a deep breath and looked back up toward the ceiling.
It's bad isn't it? he breathed.
You're doin' fine but just let me work on this 'til they get here.
It feels so cold. All the air hitting . . .
    Just try to breathe steady, Parker. Let's try and get you
comfortable 'til they take over.

I took my flannel off, bunched it up and got it under his head. I
held his arm upward and the new towels started to fill up with
blood. The sirens were on us now. The ambulance parked in
front of the house, loud engine running, lights banking off all
the houses across the street. Two EMTs, a blonde fire hydrant of
a girl and a tall, dark-haired man, emerged and without a word
streamed into the garage and started tending to Parker.

We'll take it from here, the girl said.
    He your son? She motioned toward Ben.
    Yeah, I said. He's our son.
    Take care of him, she said.
    I'm Kim and that's Felix. We're with Three Rivers and we'll
get him to the emergency room as soon as we've got things stabilized here.

She went and kneeled down next to Felix, who'd already begun
replacing the towels with proper dressings. He was fast and
confident, and they talked low as they each moved along with

their duties. All seemed some umbilical, unspoken, flat line between them.

I went over to Ben and took him by the arm and shoulder and helped him upward. He leaned against the garage door frame and spit out toward the yard. A glow of sweat showed on his forehead and soaked his hairline. He'd gone pale and his eyes stared off toward the row of houses across the street. I wrapped my arms around him and held him for a minute, but his arms lay straight down. He was shaking and I could feel the relief of his spine across my forearms. Kim and Felix softly asked Parker questions behind us, bandaging his wrist and palm. I could hear Parker pausing, then responding in whispers. I pulled back and looked up to Ben.

Hon, I know you're shook but I need you to tell me how it went down.

Only heard a slam on the other side of the wall. I was just in my room. I had my headphones on and there was a loud grunt and I pulled 'em off and ran out.

Ben's lip quivered.

Was it a fit?

I think so, mama. I mean, I only really dealt with that one at the floodways, but the look in his eye when I came out was like he wasn't there. Like the look on his face I saw on the banks.

I think I know, honey.

I'm scared, Mama. What if I wouldn't a' heard? What if there was no slam and I just didn't know?

Honey, it's all right.

He coulda died out here and I wouldn't have even known. Just a few feet away.

Ben fell back into my arms and this time he hugged me tight.

I never figured I could look after him on my own. I was always scared something like this might—

They're gonna get him to help. I said.

I looked back to Kim and Felix. They still moved steady and they'd stabilized Parker. They both rose up and went down the driveway to get the gurney. As they unloaded it from the ambulance, Ben leaned hard on the doorframe, reaching up for more balance. Still staring off across the street.

You think he's gonna be all right, Mama?

I quickly picked up the bloody towels and the flannel off the garage floor. I grabbed a trash bag off the shelf, shoved them down into it. Knotting up the bag I walked back over to Ben.

I think he's gonna be all right, hon. I said.

They rolled the gurney into the garage. They were able to get Parker to sit up, and eventually stand for a moment. They sat him on the gurney, laid him back and secured him. They rolled him out across the driveway and the lights glanced off his tired face and the trees above as they loaded him into the ambulance. The diesel engine still rumbled and the red and blue lights bounced off the surrounding houses and trees. Two neighbor boys, maybe four and six, looked on with their mama from their yard across the street.

You all can follow us, Kim said. Or if you know where you're going . . .

We know where we're going, I said as Ben and I got into Mo's car.

Parker

Melinda and I always tried to go on nights that weren't Nookie Night. Nookie Night was usually the weekends, when the place was packed and folks got real drunk and frisky. We always went on weeknights when the lines were shorter and maybe when there'd be no one in the room next to us. Could park close and not have to have valet or haul things too far. Go when most of the slot machines we liked were open. Less competition and fuss if we wanted in on poker. Would always try to get something sweet for Ben, for when we got back home. Something to let him know we were thinking of him. But Mama and I, we liked to have our space. Our time. Pick a spot and let's sit a little and watch this sunset. I got the cooler. You need something from the car? Okay, hon. You chill. That's the way it was when we got away from dishes and lawns and chores and leaks and mail and bills and phones and schedules. That's the way it got when we got to clear our heads, even for just a little bit.

I felt the rumble of the town streets under the ambulance, and I could just make out the voices of the EMTs. Bright-ass box on wheels. Do they know how this looks? Could they know? I felt their overworked and calloused hands on my forearm. In those hands I sensed their long hours and tireless ways. I wondered if they had kids waiting at home. Then what? Car payments? School? They'd train elsewhere. Maybe be from far away, then be shattered to have to work a town like this. Old friends they'd write to, having to explain this place.

We'd valet from time to time. They said it was free, and it was. But it was always nice to leave something. A tip for a kid working hard. I'd go get the first round. Melinda'd go on about Damn The Torpedoes, and then me about Hard Promises.

You're fucking kidding, she'd say. Against Refugee, Even The Losers and Here Comes My Girl? she'd say. You have no argument beginning and ending there, she'd say.

And I'd take a long drink and look away and the second I did she'd know she was right and of course I would too even though no one loved The Waiting like me. Then I'd go get the second and third rounds and I'd press her about her sister and how she'd seemed stuck in Clarkton the same old way for too long, and Melinda'd push right back. She'd push right back and say I love you hon' but nothing comes between me and my sister and those are the wrong buttons to push right now on a nice night like this and when she did I'd know she was right and of course I shouldn't have pushed those buttons, but truth was I thought a lot of her sister and thought she had more to offer up in this world than those cul-de-sac office jobs that always vacuumed out her spirit and soul in Clarkton. Corrosive maybe. Dead end at least.

Out the ambulance window I could see the red lights of the all-caps EMERGENCY overhang. I sure knew it was trouble then. The driver's voice chimed in and now there were three people running the ship. Diesel engine still rumbling and being official and all. Stern faces and everyone's in control, right? Clipboards and an I.V. far as I could feel and then here's what we're gonna do. We're gonna this and we're gonna that. Back then Melinda'd say we're gonna hit the pool after this round and I'd say we're gonna play craps. She'd say no, we're gonna hit the pool after the next round and I'd say let's just get out of here. She'd say when we get to the room you get one more Bud Light but then I want sexy time. She'd say I brought good candles and oil and I want our bodies naked and next to each other in the warm light. Then she'd say I want your hands on my back and then on my stomach and then on my thighs. She'd say all of that and I'd start looking toward the stairway. When she said those things I did. And then I'd say let's get out of here and that's about when we would push our chairs back and go.

The gurney wheels rattled uncooperative underneath me. We passed through two or three sets of doors and the hallway reeked of institution cleansers and chemical lemon. The cold on my wrist from all the blood was gone now. I only felt heat at the wounds, the warmth of gauze and wraps keeping it in. New voices now. I'd been handed over and the first EMTs were probably drinking coffee in some room not far from here, or maybe they were halfway home. As far as I could tell the ambulance hadn't come that far, and all of us around here knew that actual serviceable care was at least two county lines away. The gurney stopped and they lowered me down. Now four green masks appeared and hovered above me, backlit by searing light. One mask talked about how hungover he'd been yesterday after the cookout, and another mask said Hey chief, it is what it is. 'least she went home with you. They started to open up the EMTs bandages and readied the tools for full stitching. Full repair. I slowly opened my eyes wider, and all the lights seemed even brighter and more menacing now.

Melinda

Name tag said Becky. Becky said do you have your I.D., and I said yes. She said you'll need to fill out these forms and handed me a clipboard, and I said all right. She said this is for your husband, Parker, yes? There wasn't another soul in the waiting room, so Becky's guesswork was minimal. I said no. But then I said well, yes. She said well is he your husband or not, and I said yes. She said well, go ahead and sit down and fill this out. When you're done bring it back over. Ben and I sat and I looked over all the questions. He knew I needed a pen, got one out of the left front pocket of his jeans, and handed it over without even looking at me. I still had most of Parker's information memorized. SSN, DOB, POB, Occupation, Address. No problem. Marital status, technically yes. Didn't know if he was smoking much anymore, but it was never long between quits with him, so yes. History of cancer in family, yes. Worked in a dusty job, yes. Chemical job or exposure, I think maybe. Quarry, no. Mine, no. With asbestos, I don't think. And so on. I felt pretty sure of myself until it got into deeper medical history, then family medical history. Things slowed down there.

Ben had his arms wrapped around his midsection and bent forward. A bow-tied, Campbell's Soup kid of a TV show host ranted angrily at his guest about immigration on the TV above us. I'd seen him before and recognized the voice. A boy in man's casing. White-bred boiling pot of privilege in the grips of a hot-plate anger I couldn't at all sympathize with, surely headed home to his seven-figure-priced house and twelve-hundred-count sheets. No one's got it worse than him, I said to Ben. It was so loud I couldn't decide whether or not Parker would consider himself in good health or not. I went on and checked yes. Ben sat up, grabbed the remote and cut the Campbell's Soup kid's TV show off. He's an immigrant, too, Mama, Ben mumbled. Just not locked in enough to remember it, he whispered.

Ben wrapped his arms around himself again, bent back forward, and attempted to rest. Rheumatic, diabetes, kidney, bladder problems, all no. Epilepsy, not really. But the fits, yes. I'd come back to it. Lung trouble, I don't think. Any chest illnesses in the last three years, not sure. Pneumonia, no. Bronchitis, I don't think. Hay fever, no. Emphysema, no. Heart trouble, I don't think. Blood pressure, I'm not sure at this point. Usually cough first thing? I don't know. If so have you had a cough for long? I don't know. If so, is it all day or just first thing in the morning or at night? I don't know. I turned the clipboard over and looked up at the pocked ceiling of the waiting room. I exhaled strong. Ben still rested. He didn't move. Other than us the place was still empty.

I rose and took the clipboard over to Becky. She had her head toward her monitor and waited me out a bit. She looked up and said All right now, all done? I said I filled it out as best I could. I told her Parker and I hadn't been together for a while. I told her I was just trying as best I could at this point. She said well, that's fine and what kind of insurance will we be working with here tonight? I didn't say a thing. She said do y'all have insurance? And I still didn't say a thing. I looked back over at Ben, then across all

Becky's papers. All papers for people with insurance, probably. The papers of people that had a plan. Will you be paying out of pocket, then? Becky said. I said I guess. Becky said if you or Parker have any kind of provider I'll take that info now. I said I don't think we do. She said if you want to make a call just to make sure, that's all right. I said I don't really have anyone to make a call to. She said So out of pocket it is? I said I think. How much would that be? She said well, for this kind of condition and situation it's two-eighty-five off the top for an emergency room visit, but I'll need to see what the ambulance charges are given that they're separate contractors. They're separate contractors? I asked. They'll invoice you, she said. It's a whole separate thing? I asked. It is in this county, yes, Becky said flat, looking down at her papers again. Then she looked back up and said I'm only associated with this property. So for that the charge for entry into the E.R. in this kind of situation is two-eighty-five.

I felt for my wallet in my back right pocket. I knew there wasn't a thing in there that could help this. I went for my front left pocket and pulled out the three-hundred Raylene had given me in Metropolis. The bills were wrapped in a handful of wrinkled gas and food receipts, stringing stops between Clarkton and Metropolis and back here to Rutherford together. I counted the fifteen twenty-dollar bills out on the counter and pushed them over to Becky. She reached for the money and counted it out. Becky said okay, and wrote something down on the paper to her right. Then she counted out one tattered ten and five ones. She pushed them back across the counter and said that'll be fifteen back for you.

It's late now so we'll go ahead and keep him overnight, Dr. Crawford said. He'll probably be all right for discharge come late morning. We stood outside the room where Parker was, and I remembered being in this wing when Daddy passed. The hall was dark and quiet, and Ben leaned against the wall a few feet away, exhausted. I asked how the operation went. There were two severe lacerations, Dr. Crawford said. The one at the wrist pretty deep to the bone and just missing the radial artery. If y'all'd not caught him when you did he wouldn't have had much time. We used continuous sutures on both wounds, and in all we're looking at eighty-four stitches. He's in there, stabilized and resting now. We used a local anesthetic and had to lean pretty hard on it. He's woozy, so all the rest he can get is best. Y'all can go on in. If you want to stay the night, that's fine. Chair next to the bed reclines pretty well, and that small couch against the wall pulls out. Sheets are in the closet and there's a bathroom with a shower. Tammy's your nurse tonight and she'll be in once an hour or so. I'm heading up to three right now, but I'll come back by at least once before morning.

Ben and I walked in slow, full of dread. I realized we'd brought nothing. Not even a toothbrush. The overhead light was on, and Parker slept with his head cocked to the right side. His left arm now the silhouette of a bandaged block under clean, pressed sheets. Ben sat down on the little couch. He could barely keep his eyes open. I went around and lowered myself into the chair by the bed.

Mama, what time is it? Ben whispered.
   It's 11:47, I whispered back.
   He seems steady.
   Yeah. He does.
   We gonna stay?
   I think so, hon.
   You mind if I rest a little bit, then?
   No, hon. Get the sheets. I think that thing pulls out from the side. Make it up and get some sleep, hon.
   What're you gonna do, Mama?
   This thing's not bad, I said pulling the chair out . . . I'll be all right. There an extra blanket in that closet?
   Yeah, Mama.
   Will you get that for me?

Yeah, Mama. You care if I turn off this overhead?

No, hon. We should all rest. Go on and leave that bathroom light on. Leave the door cracked.

All right, mama.

Ben made up the bed, turned off the overhead, took his shoes off and crawled under the sheets in his jeans and T-shirt.

I heard the rustling of the sheets slow down after he'd situated himself.

Goodnight, Mama.

Goodnight, hon. I said.

I laid out under the blanket. I wasn't sure how much time had gone by after a while. I'd come back in, then fallen back out. The night pushed onward but the walls and lighting and room had it to where I could no longer decipher what was sleep and what was just catnapping. As far as I was concerned it all looked and felt the same inside hospital walls. Pretty much all the time. I felt drugged from the press of days and miles, and Maureen gone. And now this. Here we all were. Together again.

We got lucky. I heard soft and slurred.

What?

Parker's head was still tilted to the right, now toward me in my chair. His eyes half open and bloodshot, words slow.

I said we got lucky.

I kept the blanket over me but turned to my left toward Parker. I folded my knees up toward me, not fully sure what to say.

How? I asked.

Him, he said. His eyes motioned over toward Ben, snoring low, then back at me.

Ben?

Strongest one of all of us, Parker slurred.

Well, I agree . . .

Strongest. None more beautiful, he whispered, looking back over at Ben.

I think so. But why do you think so? I asked.

Doesn't run.

How?

Doesn't run. You and I do. Most everyone we know does. Or has. Or seems about to. And I guess that's okay. But he doesn't.

His eyes drifted in and out.

He's a rock, Parker whispered.

I know. But he ain't seen what we've seen in life just yet.

I think he's beyond all that. He's bigger than that. Parker slurred.

He situated himself in his bed, all body parts moving except the left hand, plaster block. He looked upward toward the ceiling.

Should try a trip, he said.

A trip?

Just to see.

Just to see what? I asked.

I guess just to see, he whispered.

They gave you a lot of meds, huh?

Yeeeeah, he smiled slightly upward.

Can you feel much?

Not much on this side. Pretty fuzzy.

You want a sip of water? I asked.

I'm all right, he said.

We paused.

But maybe some short little trip, he whispered.

Table Rock or something.

Could go over to Lake Barkley. We never went there.

Maybe Bull Shoals, Parker said.

Or Norfork, I said.

Parker didn't say anything at this point. He moved his block of a left arm slightly and got his legs comfortable. No nurse came in. No Dr. Crawford. I leaned up out of my chair and took a small sip of Parker's water. I re-situated my blanket and centered myself, leaning back. I looked upward. I thought about the kind of peace a little time on the water gave a person, and counted twenty-one and a half ceiling tiles above me as Parker started to let out small snores. I wrestled my left hand free from under the blanket, then reached up under the bars of his angled, robot bed. I took his right hand in mine. Along his palm I felt the calluses of a different life. In his fingers I felt separate experiences long gone by. He slept, and by now his hand lightly squeezed mine. I turned my head the other way toward the window. The low indigo light of another day started to make its way through the blinds. Outside I could hear what sounded like a couple of robins starting up their morning songs. Maybe for each other. Or maybe just for anyone willing to listen.

Acknowledgements

Thank you to my family: Jessie, Jack, Hazel and Sonora. Thank you to Darin Bradley and Chris Welch at Goliad. Thank you to Matt White and John Moreland. Thank you to Michael Parker, Don Lee, Kathy Pories, Wiley Cash and Willy Vlautin for reading this in its various drafts and stages, and for encouraging me onward. And thank you to Rebecca Markovits and Adeena Reitberger at *American Short Fiction*.

A portion of this novel first appeared in *American Short Fiction* Volume 22, Issue 69 - Summer 2019.

CPSIA information can be obtained
at www.ICGtesting.com
Printed in the USA
FSHW021131010321
79023FS